Flower GIRLS

God will give
you strength...
turn to Him
for guidance!

♡

jclafler

THE
Flower
GIRLS

J.C. LAFLER

PRAISE FOR NOVELS BY
J. C. LAFLER

"Just finished *Love—What's God Got to Do with It?* SO GOOD! Love how the author brought in the whispers of the enemy and how he uses whatever voice will work. BOOM! So much redemption! GREAT JOB."

—Athena Dean Holtz,
publisher, speaker, author, pastor's wife,
award-winning podcaster

"J. C. Lafler has done it again! From the time I got my hands on this book, I could not put it down. It is a curious concoction of characters who capture our hearts in a Christian context.

When I read the last sentence and closed the book, I smiled and knew I would be recommending this book to many people. *The Flower Girls* will keep you on the edge of your seat and ultimately knock your fuzzy socks off!"

—Tammy Whitehurst,
speaker, writer, and codirector of the
Christian Communicators Conference

"**I**'m not an avid reader, but my mother encouraged me to read J. C.'s first novel, *Lost and Found*. I was hooked. I couldn't put it down, and I couldn't wait for her next novel. I have read each of her novels and find them to be inspiring, sad at times, but very uplifting in the end. Her novels give you hope and love, and they guide you to believe in faith when all else fails, no matter what obstacle is in your life. I purchased her first five books for my ten-year-old granddaughter, and she has read and loves every one of them."

—*Diane Coss, homemaker,*
mother, and grandmother

"**I**n a world full of negativity and turmoil, J. C. Lafler's books are a breath of fresh air. The characters come to life as we experience pain, loss, and joy right along with them. We are taken on a journey where faith, love, and hope prevail. I can't wait to read what Lafler has in store for us next!"

—*Jill Riegel, customer sales analyst*
for Dare Products, Inc.

"**W**hat a pleasure to read J. C. Lafler's books. I loved her first book, *Lost and Found*. Then I couldn't put down *Amazing Grace*. Then I learned the back story of *Amazing Grace* with *Hope Everlasting*. You won't be disappointed while enjoying this author's books!"

—*Karen Reeves, financial*
consultant for Edward Jones

OTHER NOVELS BY J. C. LAFLER

Lost and Found

Amazing Grace

Hope Everlasting

A Leap of Faith

Finding Joy

Love Never Fails

Love—What's God Got to Do with It?

Find more information about this author and descriptions of these stories at www.jclafler.com.

Published by Redemption Press, PO Box 427, Enumclaw, WA 98022.

Toll-Free (844) 2REDEEM (273-3336)

Redemption Press is honored to present this title in partnership with the author. The views expressed or implied in this work are those of the author. Redemption Press provides our imprint seal representing design excellence, creative content, and high-quality production.

ISBN 13: 978-1-951310-97-4 (Paperback)
978-1-951310-98-1 (Hardcover)
978-1-951310-99-8 (ePub)
Library of Congress Catalog Card Number: 2023904632

Have I not commanded you?
Be strong and of good courage; do not be afraid,
nor be dismayed, for the Lord your God
is with you wherever you go.

JOSHUA 1:9 NKJV

Prologue

*A*ccording to the emergency room personnel, it was one of the worst cases of abuse or torture they'd ever seen. Someone had done a real number on the poor woman. Her face looked like she'd been used as a punching bag, and the rest of her body was bloody and bruised. Her feet and legs had cigarette burns, one of her shoulders was dislocated, and there were deep gouges on her wrists and ankles, suggesting she had been restrained at some point. The flowered dress she wore was covered in blood. No one could figure out how she had made it to the hospital.

She hobbled into the emergency room at two o'clock in the morning and collapsed on the floor. "Please help me," she whispered through split, puffy lips. "Please help my babies. They're triplets."

The nurse in charge, Ann Parkinson, rushed to her side. "Hurry! Over here!"

Emergency room personnel lifted the woman's swollen, battered body onto a bed and wheeled her to surgery. Nurse

Parkinson located another nurse to cover the emergency room for the rest of her shift, then rushed to the operating theater where the woman had been taken so she could watch from above.

Somehow they managed to keep the woman alive until the three babies were removed from her grotesquely swollen abdomen. As the doctor lifted out the third tiny body, he declared that all three little girls had miraculously survived.

The woman's eye that wasn't swollen shut flickered briefly, a smile tried to form on her puffy lips, and she was gone.

Unclenching her hands, Nurse Parkinson headed to the neonatal area, where she could oversee the three newborns. This was her area of expertise, and now she knew why she had felt compelled to cover the emergency room when another nurse asked her to take this shift. God always had a plan, and she was thankful she had listened.

The babies shared one bassinet, enclosed in a sterile unit with tubes and wires going in every direction. Their heartbeats and vitals were monitored on a screen, but they lay still, with only an occasional twitch or almost inaudible squeak to register visible life. Each of their bodies weighed between three and four pounds, which was great for a set of triplets, but they had a long road ahead of them to get anywhere near normal weight. Especially without their mama.

"Poor little orphans," Ann whispered. "Yet somehow your mama got here to save you, despite being beaten almost to death. Better off in heaven than here, I say. God rest her soul. What kind of person hurts a pregnant woman like that?"

When Nurse Parkinson told the nurses in the unit that the girls' mama had worn a flowered dress, they gave each of the girls a flower name. So Lily, Violet, and Rose continued to thrive in spite of the violence that had taken their mama in the early-morning hours of their birth.

A month later, she marveled again at the three little girls, now in a larger shared bassinet. They had almost doubled in size. Other nurses had tried separating them once they were disconnected from most of the monitors, but when they took one out for bathing or feeding, she cried until she was back with her sisters. It was amazing how being together seemed to comfort them.

Ann had asked for a piece of the woman's dress before they buried her. She had laundered it and cut it into three strips of material, then made a small tube out of each piece that she stuffed lightly with cotton. She attached a loop of ribbon at the end of each that snapped together, perfect for attaching a pacifier or small toy. Later on it would be a memento for the girls from their mother. There was a bright pink ribbon for Rose, deep purple for Violet, and white for Lily. The press affectionately nicknamed them the Flower Girls, and everyone in the community followed suit.

As far as Ann knew, no one had come forward with any knowledge about the woman who had passed—at least no one legitimate. A close friend in Child Protective Services had shared that money and offers for the triplets had poured in from across the state. So far, the offers were to take one of the infants and raise them. CPS held out, hoping to find a home that would take all three and keep them together.

But time was running out. The top three candidates were in the investigation process, and unless someone else came forward soon, they would likely be considered. At Ann's urging, the hospital had already kept them longer than necessary, and although it was a unique situation, they would be released as soon as CPS approved the adoptions.

For an instant the thought of keeping all three infants herself popped into Nurse Parkinson's head, but looking around the neonatal unit, she pushed it aside. It had taken years to get where she wanted to be at the hospital, to care for just these kinds of babies. She was needed here and would not be able to continue with three children in tow. Still, she would never forget the Flower Girls, nor would they be forgotten by the small Texas hospital and the surrounding town.

Detective Dan Baxter had been with the Texas Police Department for over ten years. He was called in to cover the case when the hospital reported the death of a severely beaten pregnant woman. He followed the trail of blood she left behind when she hobbled into the hospital that early June morning. It took him across the emergency entrance and a nearby sidewalk, but at the street it disappeared. His first thought was that she'd been dumped out of a car and left on her own.

Several days later, he talked to Margaret, the new manager of Home Town Library, where the woman had been kidnapped.

"Like I told the other cop who was investigating the murder here, the manager at that time, Janice Miller, was pregnant, and I was planning to relocate to this branch when she had the baby. She planned to stay home with him, and I'd agreed to be her replacement. Unfortunately, she was shot and killed that night trying to stop the kidnapping."

"So the woman who was kidnapped wasn't employed by the library?"

"I don't think so. I didn't know her at all."

"Thank you, Margaret." He handed her his card. "If you think of anything else, give me a call."

A month later, he was still perplexed. After speaking with person after person, he was no further along. How could a severely beaten woman who had managed to hobble into the hospital and deliver three infants before she took her last breath leave nothing behind? Where were her family, friends, and husband?

The story had been in the Del Rio paper, a tiny article under a picture of the three babies. Two women and a man had come in at different times, claiming they were friends or relatives and would take the babies, but none of them could provide any proof of the connection or even the name of the woman. Their claims were dismissed.

Detective Baxter visited the triplets once a week. He always left with renewed determination to find the person responsible for killing their mother, but so far nothing had shown up.

He had barely made it back to the office after one such visit when his phone rang. "Detective Baxter."

"Are you the cop investigating the mother who died after she had triplets?"

"Yes." He could barely hear the voice on the phone. "Can you speak louder?"

Prologue

"No, man, I don't want my girlfriend to hear me. She doesn't think I should get involved. Could we meet somewhere? How about that café at the corner of Tenth and Center Street? There's a picnic table out back. Give me twenty minutes."

"I'll be there." He picked up his badge and headed out. It was probably a long shot, but it was worth listening to what he had to say. Assuming the guy showed up.

CHAPTER 1

The Top Three Candidates

Alberta Rhodes

Alberta Rhodes lived on the outskirts of Houston with her husband, Charles. Almost six feet tall, she was dishwater blond with a narrow face and small features. Meeting Charles had been a relief after almost always being taller than the men she dated, and next to his six-foot-three frame, she thought her tall, slim build looked pretty good.

They had the perfect family and lifestyle. Their son, James, was six, and their little girl, Jasmine, was three. Alberta gave up her career as a dentist after their children were born. Charles was a lawyer and a recent partner at his firm. He was notorious for taking on criminal cases that no one else wanted, and when he got them off on a technicality, he reveled in the publicity and outrage that followed. His caseload continued to grow, and he was being looked at for a judgeship in the near future.

"Did you see the case about triplets who were born in Del Rio, Texas?" Charles asked her at dinner one evening.

"Yes. It's so sad that their poor mother didn't make it."

"Child Protective Services is looking for parents for them. They're already a month old."

"Oh, Charles, tell me you aren't suggesting we take on triplets? Jasmine is almost ready for preschool, and I was hoping to go back to work soon. Dentists are in short supply right now."

"Not all three of them. But I was thinking about offering to take one of them. It's not like we need you to go back to work. Wouldn't you like to have another baby without having to go through a pregnancy?"

"Not really." She dropped her silverware and pushed back her chair. "I finally have two children who are potty-trained and somewhat self-sufficient. Why would I want to go through all of it again? Besides, we already have a boy and a girl. I thought we were going to stop at two."

"Well, that's pretty selfish." He went on chewing, pointing his fork at her. "What about the poor little orphans who desperately need a home? They have no one to take care of them. Their mother is dead and no one knows who their father is. Do you realize the publicity we'd gain for adopting one of them?"

"Publicity? Are you serious?" She stood, ignoring the children who were giggling as they threw peas at each other. She stalked over to her husband. "You aren't the one who'll have to take care of her. You always expect me to do everything that goes along with raising a child while you continue on as if nothing has changed. I don't think I want to sign up for that again, especially with someone else's child."

"We can hire a nanny. I think we should at least consider it." He seemed unconcerned about the emotion that was building inside her, and for once his very striking dark hair and eyes did not distract her.

He pushed away from the table and stood, looking down at her. "It would put us in a good light with my partners and might be just the thing I need to get the judgeship coming up. Do you realize what that would do for my career? The sky would be the limit, and we could have and do anything we want. Think about the future instead of yourself. I'll see if I can get more information on applying for one. I really think we should do this. By the way, I didn't care for the seasoning on the steak. Ask the cook to use something different next time. I'll be in the den. I've got some paperwork to catch up on."

Alberta's hands went ice cold as she twisted them together. Her head pounded and she felt almost ill. Take on another baby? How could he just dismiss how she felt about that? And what would their kids think about it? Their parents? Maybe Charles would forget to look into it. Or maybe she would look into it herself and find a reason it wasn't possible.

"James and Jasmine, stop that right now. Go to your rooms." She spoke louder than she intended to, and both children scrambled from the room.

She rubbed her hands together and shook off a headache as she left the table and headed upstairs to get the children bathed and ready for bed. She would make sure they were fast asleep before she got on her computer. Charles hated having to deal with the children when he had work to do.

Victoria Taylor-Mason

Victoria Taylor-Mason had always wanted a child and was thrilled when her husband, Randall, shared her desire for children. But it just wasn't in the cards for them. After four years of trying and four miscarriages, the doctor advised her to consider alternatives to natural birth, suggesting adoption, a surrogate, or in vitro.

That had been two years ago, and she hadn't been able to convince her husband to consider anything. Not being able to conceive made her feel like a total loser, and she was pretty sure he felt the same way. Sometimes she caught him looking at her sourly, and he wasn't as playful or loving as he had been when they first married. She knew he wanted a big family like his own, and he would never have that with her.

The nursery they had prepared in their beautiful new home sat empty. If he would only consider one of the other options, but he wasn't interested in looking into any of them, and he didn't even seem to be very interested in her anymore, although she was in the best shape she had ever been in and worked hard to stay that way. The beautiful strawberry-blond hair, hazel eyes, and slight frame made her naturally attractive, and Randall had once raved about her beauty. But he didn't seem to notice anymore. Victoria felt their dream of children disappearing.

When she read the article about the triplets, hope soared inside her like a hot-air balloon. Triplets scared her a bit, but what if they applied for just one of the babies? She could fill out all the paperwork and send it in. If they were denied, Randall wouldn't even know about it.

She wrote down the website address listed in the newspaper, looked it up on her computer, and started the process of providing basic information. She'd make them look like the perfect couple to take on a baby, at least on paper.

Stevie Cortez

Stevie and Antonio Cortez had been married for five years and ran a lucrative computer programming company in Houston, Texas. They made an attractive couple, with her straight blond hair, green eyes, and light skin contrasting boldly with his curly black hair and dark skin and eyes.

When they first discussed raising children, adopting a child seemed like the best way to go since Stevie's past surgeries due to ovarian cancer made getting pregnant impossible. Two horrible years fighting the cancer, and finally beating it, had made them stronger. She knew she was blessed to have a godly husband like Antonio, and their faith through the battle had only grown deeper. But they still longed to have a child.

They had visited adoption agencies and filled out paperwork time and time again, only to be turned down. After the fourth rejection, their dream of a family was fading. The fact that they were a biracial couple seemed like a mark against them.

When Stevie read the article about the triplets, hope crept into her heart. After researching the case, tears formed in her eyes. That poor mama had been robbed of her babies, but she had managed to save them. Antonio might question starting with triplets, but what if they just applied for one of the little girls?

She got busy filling out the information. A baby girl would make their life complete. And it wouldn't hurt to mention that biracial couples should be represented in the selection process.

Detective Baxter

The area near the café was even worse than he'd imagined, with garbage and debris littering the streets surrounding the run-down buildings. The café sat on the corner of Tenth and Center, looking like a worn-out shoe that had seen better days. Baxter shook his head sadly, wondering why he had come.

He rounded the side of the building and saw a man slumped on the bench of a picnic table, furtively looking over his shoulder every few seconds.

Baxter walked up to the opposite bench and took a seat. "You called about the triplets, right?"

"Yeah. I, um . . . I think I saw her that night. The mother, that is. But look, mister, I can't get involved. You know. You can't be usin' my name or anythin'. My girlfriend would probably kick me out for just talkin' to ya. But I feel bad for her dyin' and leavin' those poor babies without nobody. And that man who was with her, he wasn't nice at all. You could see she was scared and had been cryin', but he almost shoved her into the restroom and stood right outside waitin' for her. Her belly was huge, and it looked like she could have them babies any time. I wanted to tell him to take it easy, but when he saw I was lookin' in his direction, he got real nasty. Told me to mind my own business if I knew what was good for me, before I even said a word. So I left. But I came back here to have a smoke and stood where I could see them when they came out. He had ahold of her arm and almost shoved her into the back seat and slammed the door. Then he got in the driver's seat and took off with her."

"Do you remember what kind of car he was driving?"

"Yeah, it was a black SUV. Fancy as all get-out. Had one of those cat faces in the grill."

"Do you mean a Jaguar?"

"Yeah, that's it."

"Can you give me a description of the man?"

"He was about six foot, I think. Kinda burly, you know, not fat but big. And that lady, she was real pretty and looked so small next to him. I mean, except for her belly, her pregnant and all. She had on a pretty flowered dress, and they looked so out of place together. I can't imagine them even stoppin' here."

"I don't suppose you got a license plate number?"

"I tried, but it was dark. It didn't look like a regular Texas plate, though. I think it started with the letter J and some numbers. I can't be sure. Look, mister, that's all I got, and I need to get goin'."

"Can I count on you to call me if you think of anything else? I mean, you're the only clue we've had since that night."

"I don't know anythin' else. I just hope what I told you helps you find her killer. I can't get it out of my head, ya know? I just had to tell someone. But I can't have you callin' or askin' anything about me. Ya gotta keep me out of it." He stood and swung his leg over the bench. "Just call it an anonymous tip."

He disappeared like a shadow, slinking between the buildings on the street.

"Well, you must live around here somewhere," Baxter muttered as he headed toward his vehicle.

His car was warm inside, and as he rolled down the window to get some air he heard the distinct sound of a motorcycle revving. *Shouldn't be that hard to track him down if I need to.*

He turned on the air and headed toward the station.

CHAPTER 2

Five Years Later

Lily

Lily played quietly by herself in the corner of the living room. She wrapped the small doll in her blanket and gently rocked her back and forth. When her mother was going to throw out one of Jasmine's old baby dolls, Lily had gathered her courage and asked politely if she could have it. Mother had looked down at her for a moment and dropped the doll in her lap. It had matted hair, and Jasmine had written on it with a marker, but Lily hugged it close.

"I'd better not see it on the floor anywhere or it goes straight to the garbage."

"Yes, Mother," Lily replied, answering the way she had been taught. She had learned quickly that she was not to use Mama or Mom as the others did. It was not allowed, and depending on Mother's mood, could get her sent to her room without supper. She often saw James and

Jasmine make ugly faces at her when she used the more proper name.

Back in her room, Lily hurried into her tiny bathroom to find a washcloth and scrub at the marks on the doll's face. Her room wasn't nearly as nice as Jasmine's, but it was clean and orderly and smelled like apples and cinnamon.

Nanny, who had shared the room with Lily since she had come to live with the Rhodes family, brought in things to make it nicer. Like the scented candle, the soft cotton comforters for their beds, squishy pillows, and the super-soft blanket that Lily loved. If Mother questioned anything, Nanny explained that she wasn't using it anymore.

Alberta and Charles rarely visited her room anyway, and Nanny did all the laundry. No one bothered to check whether Lily's sheets were clean, although Mother looked in once in a while to make sure everything was clean and tidy and make sure Lily's "special" dresses hung neatly in her closet. She wore them when they had to go out so she wouldn't look like the orphan she was. The dresses were plain and mostly dark in color, but Nanny said they made the beauty of her blond hair and green eyes stand out more.

She smiled at her image in the mirror, giggling as she remembered Nanny's words. "You look like a pretty lily in the middle of a field of dandelions."

Five Years Later

As if thinking about her had made her appear, Nanny came in with clean towels and winked at her in the mirror. "What are you giggling at, little girl?"

"Nothing. Just trying to clean my baby."

"Where did you get the doll, sweetie? Does Mrs. Rhodes know you have it?"

"Yes. She said I could have it if I keep it off the floor. If she finds it there, she'll throw it in the garbage."

"Well now, we won't let that happen, will we? Let me help you wash her face."

Nanny

Nanny knew Mrs. Rhodes would make good on her promise if she got her hands on the doll. She made a mental note to get Lily a new doll for her birthday. How anyone could refuse to love this little beauty was beyond her understanding. Besides being sweet-natured and obedient, she had beautiful blond hair that fell in waves to her waist, and her green eyes were hard to ignore. She knew some of Mrs. Rhodes's hostility had to do with her own daughter, Jasmine, whose mousy brown hair was thin and flyaway, in spite of everything Mrs. Rhodes did to make it different.

When they were getting ready to go to church one Sunday, Nanny had offered to help tame the locks. But

Jasmine rejected her, and even slapped Nanny's face in disgust. She knew nothing good would come of mentioning it, so she let it go.

Nanny also steered Lily away from the girl whenever possible. Any kind of disagreement between the girls, at least where Lily was concerned, would not end well. And Nanny couldn't bear to see the little girl mistreated any worse than she already was. She had cared for her since they brought her home and had come to love the child like her own.

Lily

Lily didn't understand why Jasmine disliked her. She wanted a sister to share things with, but Jasmine made it clear she wanted nothing to do with her. And Jasmine always got her way.

Lily had learned to stay quiet, because questioning anything about where she came from, or why she didn't get what the other Rhodes children did, had gotten her in big trouble. And if Father overheard, he would likely tell her how thankful she should be to be a Rhodes . . . or give her a rough shaking or even a sharp slap.

So she tried to play quietly, feeling much like an unwanted toy herself. She had Nanny and loved her with all her heart. But she listened and watched constantly for her own mama and papa to come and rescue her.

Five Years Later

Violet

Violet skipped up the steps of her school, then turned to wave to her mama. Her mama waved back and blew her kisses, and she giggled as she threw one back. Then she walked in the door, smiling at the teacher who held it open for her.

Victoria

As she headed toward her office, Victoria was amazed by the little girl who had become her daughter. She was as pretty and happy as a child could be, and Victoria marveled at her luck in adopting one of the Flower Girls. Violet's wispy strawberry-blond hair was almost the same color as her own long locks, and they both had hazel eyes. Most people never guessed that Violet was adopted.

As she walked back down the sidewalk and into the building where her office was, Victoria couldn't help but think of Randall and how different their lives could have been together. She had to admit she hadn't realized what years of miscarriages and disappointments had done to their relationship. She had been so caught up in her own feelings she hadn't seen the impact it was having on her marriage until it was too late.

Randall hadn't been pleased with her for filling out the adoption paperwork. But once they brought Violet home, he seemed okay. The more time Victoria spent with the new baby, the more he seemed to lose interest in her. But she was so happy and busy she barely noticed that he had slowly started spending more and more time at the office.

Randall came home from work one night earlier than usual. He turned on the television and seemed to be settling in. She put the baby to bed, freshened up, and headed back to the living room. "She's already sleeping, but you could go up and kiss her good night if you want."

"That's okay." He rubbed the back of his neck. "I wouldn't want to wake her."

Victoria attributed Randall's hesitation to his being unsure about what to do.

"I need to talk to you, Vicki."

Her stomach dropped, but she forced a smile. "What's up?"

"I want a divorce."

"What?" Her knees gave out and she sat abruptly on the chair across from him. "But what about our marriage?"

"What marriage? All you do is fuss over that baby. A baby I didn't want in the first place. Besides, I love someone else. I'm sorry, but it's been going on for a while. Before Violet. I tried to fight it, but I can't anymore."

"You were having an affair before we brought Violet home?"

"I thought things might be better if we started a family, but I was wrong. You spend every second with that child and there isn't room for me. I was already getting pressure from the lady I was seeing, and you made it easy."

"She's no lady—getting involved with a married man."

Randall didn't respond to the barb. "I had my attorney draw up the papers for both of us. There's no sense in spending money on two attorneys. You can have the house and everything in it, and of course your car. I just want out. I assumed you'd want to go back to your maiden name, since you insisted on hyphenating yours with mine when we got married, so I had him include that. We didn't have any children together during our marriage, so we don't have the normal waiting period required when children are involved. There are also papers to amend the adoption, so Violet will take your maiden name, and you will be her sole parent. I'll take care of sending a copy of the name change for you and Violet to the adoption agency so they're aware of the change to just Taylor instead of Taylor-Mason. The baby will never know the difference or remember me."

"Sounds like you have it all figured out." Apparently he'd been planning this for a while. She'd known something was off, but she hadn't seen this coming. Victoria's insides trembled, but she would not let him see it. "Leave the papers on the dining room table. I'll look them over and let you know when I've signed them."

Randall started to say more, but Victoria waved it away. "Just leave. Please."

He walked to the door and left. Once she heard him drive away, she threw herself on the sofa and sobbed.

That had been over five years ago. She had recovered quickly and poured herself into life with a little girl she loved with all her heart. She did everything with her, and they called themselves the V-girls. Victoria was the principal at Violet's elementary school, so now that Violet was in school, things had gotten even easier. They started their days together and went home together. Life couldn't be better.

Rose

"When are we getting a sister for me, Mama? I want one with skin like mine and yours."

"Rose, you always tell Daddy his skin is beautiful, like sweet chocolate milk."

"Okay, you're right. Then maybe we should get twins, one with each kind of skin. Would that be okay?"

"Oh, Rose, if it were only that simple," Stevie replied.

Five Years Later

Rose took her mama's answer as a possibility, gave her a quick hug, and ran outside to play on the swing set in their fenced-in backyard.

Stevie

Stevie smiled as she watched her daughter play, knowing she was oblivious to what her comments had stirred up inside her mama. She knew that eventually they would have to sit Rose down and tell her why there would be no more children. Beating cancer had made her and Antonio stronger as a couple, but the treatments had rendered her sterile. How could they tell their sweet girl that there would be no siblings?

She also dreaded having to admit to Rose that she was adopted. When she and Antonio were selected as parents for one of the Flower Girls, they agreed to keep the fact that she was one of the Texas triplets from Rose until she was eighteen and old enough to understand what had happened the night of her birth. So far, the police still had no leads, but there was always a chance they would discover who had kidnapped and tortured the poor woman.

Then there was all the money people had showered the triplets with when they were born. The three families who had adopted the girls had agreed that the money should be put in a trust fund where it could grow until the girls were eighteen. At that time, it would be turned over to them and could be used to further their education and/or provide money to live on.

Antonio and Stevie had been over the moon to finally fulfill their dream of having a family. Rose was a beautiful baby, with her dark brown eyes and dark curls. She really could have been theirs. Stevie had sent up a prayer, thanking God for the gift of their beautiful girl and asking him to give them the guidance they needed as time went on.

"A penny for your thoughts?" Antonio came in, dropped his briefcase, and wrapped his arms around Stevie, where she stood watching Rose out the kitchen window.

"Rose wants a sister—actually twin sisters, so one could have my skin and one could have yours."

"Well, our little girl knows what she wants, doesn't she?"

"Yes, she does. How do we tell her there will be no more children?"

"Are you sure you don't want to reconsider another adoption?"

"I don't know." Stevie looked up at her husband. He was her rock, and she knew he couldn't love Rose any more if she were biologically their own child. She would do just about anything for him and Rose. But another baby?

Five Years Later

"We don't have to worry about it tonight, love. Rose is only five, so we have time."

Stevie melted into her husband's arms and kissed him, acknowledging how lucky she was. God had given her a wonderful man to help her through life. She wouldn't have made it through her cancer without him. She had prayed and prayed for a child, and now they had a beautiful little girl to complete their family. It was more than enough.

Detective Baxter

Dan Baxter groaned in frustration. It seemed like every time he made headway on discovering who the dead pregnant woman was, something dead-ended the trail. Five years later, he still had next to nothing.

After talking to the anonymous man behind the café all those years ago, he had tracked down the black Jaguar that he believed was used to transport the pregnant woman. It belonged to a Mr. Maxwell, who ran a boxing club and trained young men to fight. When Baxter went to the club, he was told that Mr. Maxwell was out of the country for an unknown length of time. He checked every few weeks but had yet to find him there.

This morning, he had overheard someone at the station talking about the big man who ran the boxing club being back in Texas. Seems he had a reputation for getting in trouble. Baxter lost no time heading to the club to check it out.

As he approached the guy who fit the description of the man who was seen in the café, his hands started to feel clammy and he sensed he had something. He walked as calmly as he could over to where the man was pounding on a punching bag. Baxter wasn't in uniform, but his badge was clearly visible on his jacket.

"Need something?" The man punched the bag even harder.

"You were seen with a woman in a flowered dress about five years ago. What can you tell me about her?"

"I have no idea what you're talking about. I don't know anything about a woman in a flowered dress, and I have no idea what I was doing five years ago."

"What about a pregnant woman? You couldn't have missed that. And where's the black Jaguar you owned?"

"I sold it. Not that it's any of your business. I don't know this woman you're talking about, and I got work to do. It would be best if you leave. Now." He towered over Baxter and nudged him toward the door.

Baxter looked up at the man, who was obviously trying to intimidate him. He'd had plenty of practice dealing with bullies during his fifteen years on the police force, even those significantly bigger than him. He stood his ground until they were almost touching. "No need to get defensive, I'm just following up on a lead."

Maxwell backed off, swearing under his breath.

"You have a good day now." Baxter walked out the door and got in his vehicle. The menacing man obviously knew something. Baxter would have to do some more research on the fight club and Mr. Macho Maxwell.

Unfortunately, his research didn't uncover anything more that would connect him to the pregnant woman.

When the triplets were adopted, his boss had pressed him to close the case, but he talked him into leaving it open and working on it when time allowed. That was almost five years ago, and now even he was almost ready to call it a cold case.

As he perused five years' worth of possible leads, he came across the report he had requested on black Jaguars purchased or sold in Texas from June of the year the triplets were born until now. He jerked upright when he saw something he hadn't noticed before. One of the Jags sold was missing a sold date. He picked up his phone and called Jake.

"Why would that date be missing on the paperwork?"

"I can think of a few reasons. Either the person selling the car didn't want the date when he delivered the car recorded, or the car was sold but not delivered, or the car was never actually sold."

"Really?"

"Could be the man wanted it back from whoever took it. He may have gone through the process of recording it to draw attention to the fact that he no longer owned it. You wouldn't believe the lengths some people go to with things like this. Let me take another look and see if I can find anything else. Just email me the info."

"Will do. Thanks." He hung up and sent Jake the info he had requested. "Well Mr. Macho, where did you hide that black Jaguar?"

A couple of days later, he opened his email and found a message from Jake. Attached was a picture of a note with "del. to Mex" on it. He quickly gave his friend a call. "The car was sold to someone in Mexico?"

"Looks like it. I found the message on a Post-it that had fallen out of the folder. That's what I sent you a picture of."

"The whole thing is a little odd."

"I agree. I've never seen paperwork like this before, with notes attached and everything faded. I don't know, maybe someone spilled something on it or it got wet somehow. Sorry I can't give you more, man."

Five Years Later

"No worries. This is more than I hoped for. Thanks a lot, Jake."

After he got off the phone, Baxter looked at a map and searched for towns on the border of Texas and Mexico, noting that Del Rio was one of them. Why would there be a note on the paperwork for that particular vehicle? The exact kind of vehicle that was somehow connected to the kidnapping of a pregnant woman in a flowered dress, who later had triplets and died. And—the same vehicle driven by a man who fit the description of the fight-club owner. Maxwell had to be involved. And now the vehicle seemed to have disappeared, with a note that insinuated it had been delivered to Mexico. Could someone have messed up the paperwork on purpose?

He had worked with Mexican police officers in the past—some good, some not so good. But maybe he'd take a drive over the border and see what he could find out. He had a hunch there was more to the missing Jaguar than anyone wanted him to know.

At the border office, Baxter found the agent in charge. Squaring his shoulders, he flashed his badge as he cut to the front of the line at the counter. "I'm Detective Baxter with the Texas Police Department, and I have a couple of questions. Could we sit down and talk somewhere?"

"This is fine. What can I help you with?"

The man was small, with greasy black hair and a mustache that was twisted at the ends. With his nose in the air, he made it very clear that he was not happy about being bothered.

"I'm looking for a black Jaguar that was sold sometime in the past five years. I think it was delivered here in Mexico. I believe it belonged to a Mr. Maxwell. Any of that sound familiar?"

"There are dozens of border officials who work here, and you want to know if I remember a particular car that was brought across the border sometime in the past five years? You must be crazy."

"Well, since Jaguars aren't everyday cars, I thought I might get lucky. Are there others here I could talk to?"

"Your luck just ran out, *detective.*" The border official sneered. "Why don't you turn your police car around and go back where you came from. And don't come back without the proper paperwork for a request."

Knowing he wasn't going to get what he needed, Baxter nodded at the man and left. He'd be back, though, armed with that paperwork.

At the station, the chief was waiting at his desk. "Baxter, what's this about you confronting a Mexican border official today?"

Five Years Later

Wow, news travels fast.

"Well, sir . . ." Baxter composed himself as he tossed his jacket over the back of his chair. "I had some time to work on the case of the triplets, so I was checking out a lead on the car used in the kidnapping."

"Without the proper paperwork?"

"Guess I thought I might find someone willing to provide information without it."

The chief's eyebrows rose. "This case has eaten up your time for five years and there might not be any more information. I don't need you stirring up trouble with Mexico over a case that has gone cold. Understand?"

Baxter argued with his chief for almost an hour, but it was clear he wanted to be done with all this. As far as the chief was concerned, the triplets had all been adopted and the hubbub had died down. Case closed.

CHAPTER 3

The Growing Years

Lily

Nanny was sent away when Lily turned seven, and Lily thought she'd die. But Nanny took a job at her school, so they could still see each other often. At least while she was in elementary school.

When Lily was eight and Jasmine eleven, Lily woke up one morning and felt something sticky creating big clumps in her hair, from her shoulder all the way to the ends. Someone had put big gobs of chewed, bright-pink bubblegum on her head while she was asleep. Although she knew there was only one person who hated her enough to do it, she stood silent as Mother scolded her.

"Why would you go to bed with gum in your mouth? Do you know what that does to your teeth? Where did you get bubblegum in the first place? You must have chewed a whole pack to get this much in your hair. I forbid you to have any gum in this house, do you understand?"

"Yes, Mother." Lily had learned that calling out Jasmine for the mean tricks she played on her did no good. Even if she suspected the truth, Mother would never admit it in front of Lily.

"I'm going to have to call the girl at my salon and see if she can fit you in. You'd better hope she can. You're going to look pretty silly going to school like this."

Lily's beautiful blond waves were cut very short. If that wasn't bad enough, Jasmine snorted behind her hand every time she passed.

Lily was also chastised by Father at dinner that night.

"For the life of me, Lily, why can't you appreciate all that we do for you? Do you always have to be the center of attention? You can go to bed without dessert tonight, since you had all that sweet, sticky gum last night. I can't even look at you. Just go to your room now."

Lily left the rest of her dinner and went to her room. As she looked in the little mirror in her tiny bathroom, warm, salty tears slowly trickled down her face.

Her hair grew back quickly and life went on. She learned to lock her door at night and focused all her energy on getting top grades in school. Alberta and Charles could not refute that she excelled, and even they had to admit she was gifted.

Due to Father's position in the court and his insistence that they present a high social image, all three kids went to a private Catholic school. It almost made Lily ill when Mother and Father came to school for awards banquets or conferences and acted like they were proud of her academics. They told all her teachers she was such a blessing to them.

Lily had come to know Jesus at the school and accepted him as her Savior in junior high. Nanny had always prayed with her at night before she went to sleep, so getting to know more about the Lord made her feel closer to her as well. The Rhodes family had no input, since Christianity was a required course. Her faith had gotten her through many lonely nights, and she treasured the Bible Nanny had given her. She prayed nightly for the strength to endure the Rhodes family until she could leave.

By the time she turned sixteen, Lily's hair had finally grown back, and she knew she looked pretty. Classmates raved about her green eyes and the long blond waves that were almost to her waist again. She still felt shy around most people, but she tried to be friendly, and she sensed that teachers and classmates liked her.

Jasmine was in a rehab center for the second time, and James had his own apartment now. No one worried about what Lily was doing, as they were used to her taking care of herself. Alberta always left frozen dinners in the freezer for her to warm up when they weren't home.

No one in the Rhodes family ever said anything about her birthday. But she was used to that too. She couldn't wait to be gone from this house.

When Nanny called to wish her a happy sixteenth birthday, Charles and Roberta were out to dinner with one of his fellow judges. When Nanny found out Lily was alone, she asked if she could stop by. She brought gifts—a couple of books she thought Lily would enjoy and a new wallet with sixteen crisp dollar bills inside. She also brought a small cake that said Happy Sweet Sixteen and their favorite frozen yogurt. They devoured it together in the kitchen, making sure every crumb and any sign that they had been there was removed.

After Nanny left, Lily got ready for bed and started reading one of her new books, thrilled that she and Nanny had gotten to spend time together.

Despite the way she was treated by her adoptive family, all she really wanted was to get out from under their control, ensure her future, and be accepted and loved. Thanks to Nanny, she knew how that felt. And thanks to her faith, Lily knew God had a plan for her.

The Growing Years

Violet

Violet could not remember a time when she had so many teenage girls and boys in her yard and house. Balloons floated everywhere, as she scurried around making sure everyone was having fun. Everything looked perfect.

Her mom and grandparents were having as much fun as the teens. Grandpa Jonas reveled in the attention of some of the boys, entertaining them with wild fishing tales. She joined some of the girls as they ran back and forth constantly checking hair and makeup in the powder room off the kitchen.

When she stopped in the kitchen after leaving a giggling group of girls, Violet found her mom and Grandma Marge fluttering around, arranging and rearranging every little thing. "Stop fussing, you two. Everything is perfect." She gave them a big group hug.

"You're our pride and joy, honey," Mom said, "and we want everything just right for you."

Violet grinned and went back out with her friends, knowing how much she was loved.

After games and presents, Violet looked on in awe as her mom brought out a beautiful, three-tiered cake she had made and decorated herself. Purple violets cascaded down from the top and pooled around the base, with sixteen candles scattered from top to bottom.

"Violet, come blow out the candles."

"Oh, Mom, I'm too old for that."

"Nonsense." Grandpa Jonas pulled her toward him. "All those candles are going to start a fire, young lady. You better get over there and blow them out quick."

"Oh, Grandpa, don't be silly." She leaned over the cake as everyone shouted, "Happy birthday," filling the kitchen with commotion and laughter.

After the last plate of ice cream and cake had been devoured, and the giant panda piñata full of candy busted open by the birthday girl, the party ended and parents started arriving to pick up the guests. Once the last of Violet's friends had gone, her grandparents, who had been handling clean up duty, said their goodbyes in the driveway and hugged their birthday girl one last time.

"See you later, alligator." Grandpa threw kisses toward them.

Violet smiled at the childhood game they always played. "After 'while, crocodile. I love you, Gramps. Thanks for everything." She threw a kiss back at him as he headed toward the car.

"You bet. I wouldn't have missed it."

Grandma Marge hugged her tight. "I can't believe you're already sixteen. Where has the time gone?"

Violet squeezed her hard. "I can't stay little forever, you know."

"But I wish you could, sweet girl. I love you, honey."

"I love you more."

"Thanks for having us." She got in the car and waved at her daughter and granddaughter as they stood arm in arm in the driveway.

Later that evening, the V-girls sat on the couch, talking. "It was a wonderful party. Thank you, Mom. It's always nice to have Grandpa and Grandma over. They're so good with my friends."

"Yes, they are. And speaking of friends, who was that cute boy with the dark curls and blue eyes . . . Isaiah? He seemed pretty interested in you."

"Oh, Mom."

They both laughed.

"What about you, Mom? Are you happy? I always thought you might remarry someday. Whatever happened to Michael? He seemed to think a lot of you."

"I don't know. I just can't seem to find a man who really excites me. Maybe it's just meant to be the V-girls. Or perhaps when you're off to college, I'll want to date more. Right now I don't want to miss a single minute of you growing up. I love you so much, kiddo."

"I love you too, Mom." Violet put her arm around Victoria and pulled her close, kissing her cheek.

"Did you get everything you wanted for your birthday, honey?"

"Yes, I did, Mom. Everything was perfect."

Rose

"Come on, Rose, we'll be late for our reservation. You might want to bring a sweater in case it's cold in the restaurant."

"Coming, Mom. I'm trying to find my shoes. Oh, here they are." Rose pulled on her pretty silver sandals and grabbed a white sweater off the hanger in her closet. She stopped and glanced in the mirror. Her dark eyes sparkled and dark brown curls cascaded down her back. She loved her hot-pink dress with the silver band at her waist that matched her sandals.

She hurried down the winding stairs as her mom opened the door to her best friend, Simon, who lived next door.

"I hope you're both hungry," Mom said. "Antonio made reservations at the Waldorf, and their food is amazing."

"Oh, I love it there!" Rose gave her mom a hug and then grabbed Simon's hand and pulled him inside.

He handed her a bag. "I brought you a birthday gift. Mom said I had to."

Rose punched him lightly on the shoulder as she took the gift. She opened the present to reveal a small black box. As she lifted the lid, she gasped at the delicate silver bracelet of tiny elephants that rested on a bed of cotton. "Oh Simon, it's beautiful. Can you help me put it on?"

"I know how you love elephants," Simon told her as he took out the bracelet and fastened it on her wrist. "And keep the little card underneath. It has a picture of the baby elephant that was adopted in your name."

Touched by the gift, Rose wrapped her arms around him. "You're the best friend ever, Simon." She smiled at her mom over his shoulder.

"Well, come on. We're meeting your dad at the restaurant. Let's get going."

Rose was so happy she could hardly contain her excitement as she and Simon followed Mom into the garage. They chatted about this and that as they made their way to the restaurant to celebrate her sixteenth year. All the way there, she marveled at what a lucky girl she was.

When she caught a glimpse of her mother looking back at them with apprehension, goose bumps ran up and down her arms.

Detective Baxter

Still recovering from a cold, Baxter wished he'd taken another sick day by the time he got to the office. After stowing his lunch and hanging up his jacket, he sat down heavily at his desk. He reached into a drawer and grabbed the bottle of pain tablets he kept there, already sporting a throbbing headache. As he put the bottle back, he noticed a piece of paper, folded in half, stuck under the corner of his desk calendar. When he unfolded it, the words scribbled on it sent him instantly into alert mode.

I have info on the woman who had those triplets years ago. Call 777-714-9798.

He grabbed it, hurried out of his office, and stopped at the desk of a fellow policeman. "Hey, Joe. Have you seen anyone unusual hanging around this morning? Or noticed anyone stop by my office?"

"Nope. It's been real quiet. I brought in donuts. They're in the breakroom if you want one." Joe took a big bite of an apple fritter and turned back to his computer.

Scratching his aching head, Baxter headed back to his office and dialed the number.

"What?" The raspy voice sounded female.

"I'm Detective Dan Baxter. Did you leave me a note?"

"Maybe. Can you meet me in back of the old train station?"

"Yeah. What time?"

"Give me thirty minutes." The phone clicked off.

After sixteen years, he couldn't believe anyone even remembered the case. Why would they come forward now? He went through a couple of things on his desk, then grabbed his jacket and headed back out. He was only about ten minutes from the train station, but he wanted to see who the person was and what they were driving.

He parked near the woods behind the old train station, which hadn't been used for decades, and watched for her to drive in.

A tap on the passenger window made him jump. Gathering his wits, he rolled down the window.

"You gonna make me stand out here or can I get in?"

"Sorry. I was expecting a car." He unlocked the door so she could climb inside.

"I rode my bicycle and hid it in the bushes." She coughed harshly.

"Sorry. Left over from a bad case of pneumonia. It really took its toll on me, you know? After all the risks I've taken in my life, that's probably going to be the end of me. But don't worry, I'm not contagious. It happened months ago."

"Can't you do anything about it?"

"I don't have insurance or money."

"Why did you call me after all these years?"

"I don't know how much time I have left, and I thought someone should know about Clara."

"Clara?"

"The mother of the triplets. I was in that hellhole in Mexico with her the night before she died. I helped her escape, and I escaped myself. I knew those monsters would kill me if I so much as whispered a word. So I changed my name after she died and stayed quiet. You saw what they did to her, right? It was horrendous. I can still hear her screams and the sound of them punching her, slapping her, even burning her with cigarettes. I was terrified."

"Why were you there that night?"

"They hired me a few months before and gave me a room in the basement. I was in a tight spot with the authorities and needed a place to lay low. My job was to look after the troubled girls they brought in. They said it was only until they had their babies and could go back home, but I heard and saw plenty. Those girls were never going back home. I was there to feed and watch over them. One night, a pregnant girl delivered her baby—a sweet little boy—but I don't think she ever saw him. I held him while the men loaded her in the car and placed a basket in the back to put him in. They told me they took them both to the hospital, but I know better. The girl had a hard time delivering the baby, and they probably just got rid of her." She made a slicing motion across her throat.

"You mean they killed her?"

"Either that or left her somewhere in the sticks where no one would find her in time to stop the bleeding. I'm telling you, those men had no regard for the girls' lives. They just wanted the babies to sell. They barely bought me enough groceries to feed everyone. Then they'd bring in take out food and eat it themselves. They knew we could smell the food. They laughed about it. If we were lucky and they didn't eat all of it, I would feed the scraps to the girls."

"Tell me more about Clara."

"When they brought her in, she had on a pretty flowered dress and her face was stained with tears. The big guy—Max, I think—had spotted a pregnant woman at the library and called to tell them about her, but then decided things were getting hot and he wanted out. I was at the bottom of the stairs and heard the phone conversation. They were mad as hatters and told him he had better deliver the girl first or he'd be the next one who disappeared."

"What happened when he showed up with Clara?"

"It was obvious she wasn't the woman they expected. Max told them it didn't matter, they were getting three for one because she was having triplets. He wanted to pick up his money and leave, but they had no plans to let him go. I had heard them talking just that morning about taking the girl and the car and getting rid of him. Then they'd lie low after they sold the babies. I figured they wouldn't let me live either, or they would have made sure I didn't hear about what they were doing. I mean, my room was right across from where they had Clara tied up. I knew it was time for me to leave."

"And did you?"

"That night seemed to go on forever, but eventually Clara passed out. I heard the men talking about getting something to eat. When they went upstairs, I thought I might be able to get away, but when I started out of my room, they were all in the kitchen. Their lookout man must have brought them some food. I heard all three of them talking and laughing, bragging about getting three for one *and* the car. They sent the third man back out to check on Max and do the job. I figured he was a goner."

"What happened next?"

"When they got downstairs, they tried to bring Clara around with smelling salts. I could see it all through the crack between the wall and my door. Before she was completely conscious, they told her they were going to cut the babies out of her stomach once her water broke. Then I heard the lookout yell, 'He's getting away!'"

"Max?"

"Yeah. The two men in the basement ran upstairs to go after him. That gave me the opportunity I needed. I untied Clara and we made a run for it. I practically carried her out the back door of the basement. She was barely conscious and kept telling me her babies were coming. I knew the men had chased the big guy down the driveway out front because I could hear them cussing and swearing. When I heard a gunshot, I dragged Clara into the bushes behind the house to an old wagon with wooden sides I'd found and hidden there. I helped her in, and we took off like the devil himself was after us."

"Why did you have a wagon hidden there?"

"I'd gone back and forth between Mexico and Texas for years, and I'd learned how to keep a low profile. I had friends who knew how to get across the border and disappear, and I always had an escape plan. I would have used the wagon for my belongings, but after everything that happened that night, I decided I would take Clara instead. I didn't have anything that mattered as much as her life and those babies.

I'd called a girl I knew and asked her to leave a car for me in a place that only the two of us knew about. Told her I didn't care what the vehicle looked like as long as it would get me to the closest hospital. Afterward, I would leave it at a designated spot where she could pick it up. I knew I could trust her to make sure there weren't any traces of us using it."

"What did you do when you got to the car?"

"I got Clara into the back seat of the rusty old thing and covered her up with a blanket that I found inside. I threw the wagon in the trunk and drove as fast as I could to a hospital just across the border. I couldn't go in with her, though, so I put her on the sidewalk in front of the emergency room entrance. I think her shoulder was dislocated, because she gasped when I touched it. When I tried to put her arm around my neck to help her stand, she whimpered. I told her the hospital would help her with her babies. While she stumbled toward the door, I jumped in the car and took off. I left the car in a spot near the woods where I said I would and walked to a run-down shack deep in the woods that nobody knew existed. My friend had already stocked it with food and clean clothes. She told me she'd burn the wagon and get rid of the car so nobody would trace it to me."

"Good friend."

"I watched the papers, when I could get one, and about a month later I saw the babies in an article about the Flower

Girls. I knew then that Clara hadn't made it, in spite of all my efforts, but at least the babies had. She would've been happy about that."

The woman started coughing again. "I still have nightmares about that horrible place."

"Can you tell me how to get there or the name of it?" Apprehension sent shivers up his spine when he thought about his chief's last words to him, but he shook it off.

"The men who hired me called the place a pregnancy clinic. It was just over the border of Mexico, hidden by brush and squalor so no one would notice it or come near it. A trail into the woods runs parallel to an overgrown railroad track, along a row of pine trees. There are six huge pines in a row in one spot, and you cut into the woods through the middle of them. You'll see a two-lane rough track that should lead you to the area."

She shuddered. "I can't wipe the images of those poor Mexican girls out of my mind, especially the last one. They had no idea what was going to happen. The men threatened them and told them they would find them and kill them and their families if they ever said anything to anybody. Clara was the last straw. She was big-as-a-barrel pregnant and they tortured her for hours."

"Do you think they were looking for more information on Max?"

"Yes. They asked her where his business in Texas was, and she told them over and over that she didn't know and that she'd never seen him before he kidnapped her. They didn't believe her." The woman stopped for another bout of coughing.

"What do you think the chances are of that place still being there?"

"I heard from a girl who heard from a friend of hers that it caught fire and burned down. Good riddance, I say."

He glanced at his phone. "I forgot to mention I've been recording you."

"I saw. It's okay. I owe it to that poor woman to tell the truth about what happened that night."

"No one stepped forward to claim the babies when Clara died. Do you know if she had a boyfriend, husband, or any other relatives?"

"I don't. Hopefully those little girls got good homes."

"They were all adopted. Did you ever know Clara's last name?"

"Nope. I only knew her first name because she wore a necklace that said Clara. It broke and fell off when I was getting her in the car and I stuck it in my pocket. When I read she had died I got rid of it. Look, I better get going. Don't like to stay in one place long."

As the woman opened the passenger door, Baxter jumped out of the car and thanked her for contacting him. She pulled her bike out of the bushes and hopped on. Within seconds she disappeared.

As he headed back to the police station, his head spun trying to piece together everything the woman had told him. At least he finally had a name for the woman who had saved her babies. Only a first name, but it was a start.

He called his boss from the car and told him what he had learned.

"Do you have a way to validate what she told you?"

"No. But I have the number she left me at the office. I should be able to figure out where she called from."

"Okay, let's talk when you get here. I want all the details. It'll be a miracle if we solve this case after all these years."

Distracted by the news he had just received and shared with his boss, he didn't register the semi truck coming at high speed through the intersection or the burly man behind the wheel. The impact sent metal and glass flying in all directions. His car flew through the air, then wrapped around the nearest tree. He felt excruciating pain just before everything went black.

Baxter heard sirens. He felt like he was swimming in a deep pool of black tar that was so dark and heavy he couldn't get out. There were people yelling and asking if he was okay. The pain felt like a million needles stabbing him over and over and over, and he couldn't make his voice work.

"Hey, buddy, can you hear me? Hang on. We'll get you out of there."

"It's bad," the first guy on the scene told one of the policemen who had arrived. "You'll need the Jaws of Life. Here comes the fire truck now. I hope the paramedics get here soon. It'll be a miracle if he makes it."

"Where's the other driver?" the policeman asked. "I'd like a word with him."

"He already left. His semi was still drivable. I can't believe he got away with nothing more than a few cuts and bruises. He looked familiar. I know I've seen him around town."

Baxter drifted in and out of consciousness. Nothing made sense. Closing his eyes, he felt darkness pulling him down and under, and he couldn't stop it. Finally he stopped fighting and let it take him under.

A few weeks later, he heard the beeps of multiple machines as he tried desperately to come up out of the heavy fog that weighed him down. Hearing voices, he blinked a couple of times before he managed to hold his eyes open.

"He's waking up. Let's check his vitals. Dr. Walker wants him to do it gradually if possible."

He tried to talk but couldn't make his dry mouth work. Everything seemed to take a monumental amount of energy.

"It's okay," a gentle voice coaxed. "You've been out for a few weeks in a medically induced coma. Most of the stitches and broken bones have started to mend nicely. See if you can drink a little water."

A nurse came into focus. A drink of water was exactly what he needed. He tried to rise up to the straw but fell back down.

"Here, let's put your bed up to support you. Is that better?"

He nodded and managed to sip from the straw she held toward him. The cool liquid eased the dryness in his mouth and throat. "Thank you" came out like a raspy grunt. He shook his head, disgusted.

"It'll take a few hours, maybe even days, before you'll sound like yourself. You were in a car accident. Do you remember anything?"

A scene from the wreck flashed before him, with twisted metal that blended in with trees. "A little bit." He whispered the words, and it sounded a little better. But the small amount of energy he had expended exhausted him.

"That's fine," the nurse said as she lowered his bed again. "Sleep now, and we'll try again when you wake up."

The next time he woke, he tried to focus on things in the room, but everything was blurry. He kept blinking his eyes.

Someone came up to the bed and took his hand. "Are you okay, honey? Do you need anything?" His wife, Donna, sounded worried. "I'm sorry I wasn't here when you woke up the first time. I just ran to get something from the cafeteria."

"I'm glad you're here. I feel so tired, and everything is fuzzy. What's going on? I need to find my phone and get to the police station. I found evidence . . ." His voice faded into nothing and the blackness took him again.

"Nurse!" Donna shouted.

"He's okay, Mrs. Baxter. His brain can only take so much stimulation at a time. The good news is he's trying to come back. We've removed everything that kept him in the medically induced coma, and his body is doing remarkably well, but now his brain has to catch up. This will take time. Hang in there. You have been so strong through all of this, and I'm telling you, him recognizing you and speaking is a good sign. He's likely to sleep for a while now. Why don't you go home for a bit and come back tonight?"

"Okay, you're probably right. Please promise you'll call if anything changes."

"Absolutely. Try to get some sleep yourself."

Donna picked up her purse and left the hospital. In spite of what the nurse told her, she still had doubts. "Oh, God, please help Dan keep fighting to come back to me," she whispered.

CHAPTER 4

Turning Eighteen and Learning the Truth

Lily

By the end of her junior year of high school, Lily had been accepted to several colleges, both in state and out. But Charles and Alberta had insisted on the University of Houston, thinking about the difficulty and time involved in moving her out of state. Her scholarship there covered all four years, including books and living in the dorm the first year. She didn't care which college she went to; she just wanted out from under their roof.

She already had more credits than necessary to graduate, so her principal spoke to her about graduating a year early and heading straight to college. That fit her plans as well as those of her parents.

She still couldn't believe she was actually taking college classes and was finally out of the house she'd grown up in. Other than Nanny, she had no good memories there. Her dream of her birth parents showing up had disappeared long ago. She'd learned to take care of herself and knew she could always count on God to keep her safe. She felt blessed to be a child of God. The only things she took when she left the Rhodes home were the Bible Nanny had given her and the items she had bought herself.

Her dorm room was a little shabby, but her job at the college allowed her to pick up furnishings here and there. Lily had received a scholarship in architectural engineering. She had high hopes of building one of Houston's beautiful skyscrapers someday.

Time flew by, and Lily finished her first year with a perfect 4.0 grade point average, in spite of being the youngest in her class. She had talked to an academic advisor and decided to test out of some of next year's classes and get on with the engineering classes she longed for. She would work full-time at the college most of the summer, only taking time off for the tests that would allow her to finish four years of college in three years . . . then on to a master's degree and maybe even her doctorate.

Since the university only required one year of living on campus, she found a modest apartment downtown. She hoped to start her internship for experience once the new semester began. She applied with an architectural company known for the unique designs of their commercial buildings. She spent every free moment she could squeeze out in the drawing room at the college and had several unique ideas that she hoped to share with them. While her personality remained extremely introverted, she was able to speak with confidence when the topic of architectural designs arose. People often told her she seemed far older than her eighteen years.

She rarely saw anyone from the Rhodes family and had stopped being invited to any family gatherings, which suited her just fine. She only went back to the house once, and she'd found it awkward talking about what she had accomplished when Jasmine was still in and out of drug rehabs. It was obvious none of them cared about what she was doing with her life. And James kept eyeing her like he'd like to devour her. It was creepy.

So she established her own way of life, living simply and keeping to herself. If it lacked emotional connections, that was okay. She didn't have time for romance or relationships, although she got more than her share of invitations to parties and clubs. After she gave in and let a fellow student take her out, she was turned off when he tried to coax her into trying drugs and alcohol. After having to call a cab to take her home, she decided she didn't have time for dating at this point in her life. She'd just spend time with Nanny and focus on her future. There was plenty of time for dating later on.

One night she and Nanny made spaghetti dinner at her apartment.

"I love your sauce, Nanny. You have to teach me how to make it."

The woman chuckled. "How many times do I have to ask you to call me Angel?"

"I'm sorry. You'll always be Nanny to me."

"I know, sweet girl. I just want you to know that I value your friendship as an adult now. You have grown into such a beautiful young lady, inside and out. I'm so proud to call you my dearest friend."

"And I'm glad God placed you in the house where I grew up. Angel is a perfect name for you, and I will never forget all you taught me about God and about being a good person. I owe you so much, and I hope you will always be in my life."

"Of course I will. I can't even imagine life without my Lily. Now, let me tell you how I make this delicious sauce."

A few months later, Lily received a letter, forwarded by Alberta Rhodes. She tucked it away without opening it, not wanting to spoil her day. It was warm and sunny in Houston, and she was meeting Nanny for lunch. She reached the corner just as Nanny pulled into the parking lot of a small café near her apartment.

"Happy birthday, sweet girl." She hugged Lily tightly. "Do you have any idea how much I love you, child?"

"It can't be any more than how much I love you."

"Come on, you silly girl, let's sit down and enjoy your birthday lunch so we can get on with finding your birthday present."

"I'm eighteen, Nanny. Don't you think I'm a little old for birthday presents?"

"Never. This is one of the highlights of my summer. How are you doing?"

"I'm fine. I'm working full-time at the college now, and that helps a lot financially. I'm hoping to work for Hutchins and Smith to complete my intern requirements. God will provide, as he always does." She shared her plans for the next year of college, then talked about a problem she was having with some noisy neighbors who were interrupting her sleep.

After lunch they headed to the Galleria Mall in downtown Houston. Nanny always insisted on buying Lily a smart outfit for her birthday. Lily thought the mall far too expensive, but her nanny would have nothing to do with her arguments. They wandered through the stores, exclaiming over this and that until they spotted a suit in the window of the Nordstrom department store.

"It's beautiful," Nanny said. "Do you like it?"

"You know it's going to be expensive. Let's look for something else."

"At least try it on."

An hour later, Lily and Nanny came out of the store smiling.

"I think that salesclerk was a little sweet on you. He certainly was attentive, wasn't he?"

"Yes. But he was just happy because of all the money you spent. You went overboard, don't you think?"

"Nonsense." Nanny pulled her in close for a hug. "I save all year for this, and I have no one else to spend my money on. That suit looks amazing on you, and you're going to need a couple of those for interviews with these companies you're determined to work for. I can't have my best girl looking shabby, now, can I? I'm just thankful they were able to ship your suit, the blouses, and the purse to your apartment so we don't have to drag them around. Now we need to find suitable shoes to go with it."

Lily grabbed Nanny's hand. "You've already spent a fortune, Nanny. There's a frozen yogurt place in here somewhere. Let's find it and get some of that salted caramel flavor that you like. It'll be my treat."

After the frozen yogurt, they found just the right shoes to go with her new suit. Nanny made her laugh at a pair of shoes that matched the color of her new suit perfectly but had ridiculously pointed toes. They finally settled on low-heeled pumps that were smart and comfortable.

Lily hated to see their day out end. As she thanked Nanny for the tenth time and hugged her goodbye, she knew that *thankful* could not begin to describe how she felt. Nanny was like the sibling or mother Lily had always wanted, plus a friend, all wrapped up in one package.

That Sunday after church, Lily grabbed something for lunch and sat down to go through her mail. After picking up and opening the envelope Alberta had forwarded, she pulled out a second envelope addressed to her in care of Alberta and Charles Rhodes, noticing it was from the state of Texas.

She removed a single sheet of paper from the second envelope. It seemed people had given quite a sum of money to three triplets born on the third day of June 2001, popularly called the Flower Girls. Their mother had died immediately after giving birth, and no one, including their father, had come forward to claim the mother or the triplets.

This had to be a mistake. June third was her birthday, and she was born in 2001, but she was adopted and had no knowledge of triplets. She read on.

Part of the arrangement on finalizing the adoption process for each of the three girls was an agreement with the adopting parents to tell them about the circumstances of their birth when they turned eighteen. It would be up to the state of Texas to validate the claim of each girl and turn over a check for one-third of the money. If any of the girls was not validated within two years, her third would be divided between the remaining sisters. The three girls were listed only as Lily, Violet, and Rose. A phone number was provided to call and start the validation process.

Lily turned the paper over but found nothing on the other side.

There must be some mistake. Triplets? Sisters? Money?

Violet

Violet applied for and was accepted at Rice University in Houston. She knew it was a bit of a strain on Victoria's budget, but her mom had told her she'd find the money somehow. Today they were shopping for things she'd need in her dorm room.

"I don't need much, Mom. Everything is so expensive."

"Don't worry about it, Violet. We'll make it work. We're the V-girls."

"I can get a part-time job while I'm in college. And I got that scholarship for the first semester. A check should be coming any time now. In fact, I'll go check the mail right now." She gave her mom a hug and headed to the mailbox.

She came back almost skipping. "We got it, Mom! And something from the state of Texas that has my name on it, in care of you. Any idea what it is?" She handed it to her mom and opened the scholarship check. When she looked up, her mother's face had gone pale.

"Mom, what is it? Are you all right?"

"It's about your birth. I'll look at it later. Let's go. Grandpa and Grandma gave us a thousand dollars to contribute toward college, and they're going to want to know what we spent it on."

"They're the best grandparents ever. Let's go to that big mall near Sagebrush. Maybe I can get an extra outfit for college if there's enough. I still have my savings too. I have to look cool, you know."

Her mom put the letter in the pages of the novel she was reading, then threaded arms with her as they headed to the car.

"I love you, Mom."

"I love you too, honey."

Victoria

Victoria knew she had to find a time to tell Violet about her birth. It was part of the agreement when they adopted her. And the letter had mentioned sending her a check for her third of the money people had sent in when it all happened. It had to be something substantial for the state of Texas to get involved. She remembered CPS telling her that people all over the United States were sending in money for the poor, abandoned triplets . . . the Flower Girls, whose mother had died when they were born.

If she had known at the time that Randall was going to divorce her, she would have taken all three of the babies. Of course, she probably wouldn't have been one of the top candidates without him.

She'd have to tell her soon. Tears welled up as she thought about her daughter discovering that she wasn't her biological mother. Victoria turned away so she wouldn't see her tears and listened to her daughter chatting about clothes and college and boys. She had to block the letter from her mind and enjoy this day with her. Violet was *hers*, no matter what the wretched letter represented.

Later that night, after a long day of shopping and dinner at their favorite restaurant, Victoria knew she had to share the letter and the story of Violet's birth with her. Once they looked at everything they'd bought again and carried it up to her room, Violet came down in her pajamas and plopped down on the sofa with her mom.

Victoria retrieved the envelope from where she'd tucked it into her novel. She removed the letter with a shaky hand and looked it over.

"What is this? It's from the state of Texas. Did we win the lottery? We can travel around the world and spend any amount of money we want, right?"

"I have something I need to share with you about your birth and the first month of your life, Vi."

"What are you talking about?"

"Just remember that the most important thing is our love for each other. You are the whole world to me, Violet."

"Mom, you're scaring me."

"This letter states that you are one of three girls born on June third, 2001. Your mother died immediately after your birth, and your father never came forward. No one did. You were put up for adoption, and I—well, I and my husband at the time, were selected to adopt you. I didn't think Randall would consider three babies, so I only requested one. Part of the adoption included telling you the truth about your birth once you turned eighteen. People around the country sent in money, and the state of Texas invested it for the three of you. You will get one-third of the money as soon as you prove you are one of the babies. And you are." Tears ran down her face. "I'm not your biological mother, Violet, but I love you with everything I have."

"It can't be true. There's no way. We have the same hair and the same eyes."

"Violet, I am and always will be your mother. I couldn't have children of my own, and you were the answer to my prayers. You are just as precious to me as any biological child could be." She handed the letter to Violet.

She read it and handed it back to her. "No way. You've been the best mother in the world. We're the V-girls, me and you. Nothing can change that."

"You're right. Nothing can change what we are to each other. We will go through this process the same way we have tackled everything else in life . . . together."

Rose

Rose got out of bed and stretched. It was her eighteenth birthday, and she was graduating as well. Simon and his parents were coming to celebrate with them. He had graduated a year ahead of her and already had a year of college under his belt. Lucky guy! He'd gotten into the University of Texas at Austin. She had applied there, too, but so far no acceptance. Her grades weren't quite as good as his, but she still hoped she might get in. She had been accepted at the University of Houston but was holding out in case her acceptance to UT Austin came through.

Looking at her clock, she saw she had time for breakfast. She headed downstairs in anticipation of some of her mom's pecan waffles. She almost always made them for Rose's birthday.

When she reached the kitchen, she saw her mom and dad sitting at the table. There was an opened envelope with a letter in front of them, and it was obvious Mom had been crying.

Dad gave Mom a tight hug and stood up, facing Rose.

"What's going on? Is everything all right?"

"We need to talk to you, honey." Dad put his arm around Rose and led her to the table.

"You guys look like you just lost your best friend. What's going on?"

"I'm sorry this has to come right in the middle of your birthday and graduation, but we promised to share some news with you when you turned eighteen. We were going to tell you tomorrow, but this letter came today and we think you should know. This changes nothing about how much we love you and will keep loving you. We just pray you'll understand, and we think you have the right to know."

"Know what?"

Dad looked down at Mom and squeezed her hand. "We aren't your biological parents, Rose. We adopted you a little over a month after you were born. You were one of three female triplets born on June third, and your mother died after giving birth to the three of you."

"Dad, what are you talking about?" Rose sat down hard in the chair across from them.

Antonio put his arm around his wife. "Your mom had ovarian cancer a couple of years after we were married, and while she beat the cancer, the surgeries that were necessary to get rid of the cancer resulted in her not being able to have a child. When we heard about triplets needing homes, we were ecstatic. You were the answer to our prayers—our little gift from God."

Rose stared at the two people she loved most in the whole wide world. She sat at the table looking at her mother—or the woman she'd thought was her mother. "So you've lied to me all these years?"

"You're our child, Rose, in every way that matters." Mom reached for Rose's hand. "You have always been a blessing to us. Your birth mom could not have loved you any more than we do."

"What about my dad?"

"No one came forward after your mom died."

Rose tried to process her mom's words. "You said female triplets, right? So I have two sisters? All my life I've wanted a sister and you kept that from me?" Tears trickled down her cheeks.

"Oh, honey," Mom said, "we wanted to tell you, but we couldn't. Part of the stipulation in the adoption was that we tell you your story once you turned eighteen. You can read the letter that came to us today. Maybe that will help." She pushed the letter toward Rose.

Rose snatched it and skimmed it. "They want me to call and verify that I understand the situation so they can send a check. A check for what?"

Dad touched her arm. "Apparently, when people heard your story as babies, they sent in money for your support. The state put that money in a trust fund for the three of you, so it has been growing for almost eighteen years. That money will be split between the three of you."

"So the other girls are getting this letter today too? Do I get to meet them?"

"Those are questions we'll have to ask the state of Texas," Dad said. "We can do this together, Rose. We don't expect you to figure it out on your own. And if the other girls and their parents are willing, maybe we could get together so you can meet each other."

Rose looked at her parents and saw distress on their faces. She loved them so much. They had given her just about anything a girl could wish for, while teaching her about God and faith and *everything*. Her anger evaporated. No letter in the world could change that. She jumped up and went around the table to hug them, tears streaming down her face.

Silently, they held on to one another, hating the letter that threatened to change everything.

Finally, Rose looked up at them. "Please don't stop being my parents."

Detective Baxter's wife, Donna

Donna watched from the kitchen as her husband worked with the physical therapist who had become almost a permanent fixture in their home. She thought back to the day she had received the call about his accident. Had that only been two years ago?

When she got to the hospital, he was barely breathing and tubes protruded from most parts of his body. After the initial shock, she met with doctors to work on a plan of action, and they agreed to start with a medically induced coma to let his brain rest from all the stimuli pouring in to keep him alive. Those first couple of weeks had been almost unbearable for both of them, and she had begged God to keep him alive.

As his bones and body started to heal, hope grew. Still, she knew there was a chance he would not come out of it the same man she knew and loved. That didn't matter, as long as he was alive.

She had been used to her husband's long hours, work distractions, and even his stubbornness when he worked a case. But now she looked on with admiration as he put those very traits toward getting his body back to normal after the horrible accident that would have defeated a weaker man.

It would take years of almost constant work and therapy to bring his atrophied muscles back to normal, but if anyone could do it, Dan could. He was determined to get his health back and finally finish the case of the triplets. Then the real worrying would begin.

CHAPTER 5

The Years Fly By

Lily

For once in her life, Lily felt excited. As she sat among other graduates in a sea of red-and-gold caps and gowns, she twisted and untwisted the tassels on the gold sash draped around her shoulders that signified her academic excellence. Today was her graduation from the University of Houston with a bachelor's degree in architectural engineering. Her academic excellence had landed her a full-time position with one of the main architectural companies in Texas as well as a spot in an elite architectural drawing school that few even knew about.

She had a moment of intense sadness, wondering where her sisters were at this point in their lives. Violet and Rose, the sisters she had yet to meet but prayed for nightly. She hoped she would meet them someday. And she prayed for her heavenly mother, who had stayed alive until she was born.

Nanny waved madly from the crowd, and pure joy overcame the sadness. Lily knew how much God had given her, and she would forever be grateful for her precious nanny who had fulfilled the role of a mother and continued to be her dearest friend.

The music starting playing and the graduates stood, preparing to cross the stage and receive their diplomas. It had been almost a year since she had changed her name and taken Nanny's last name, becoming Lily Flora Martino, finally eradicating the Rhodes family from her life. She knew how proud it made Nanny to claim her as her own.

When her name was called, she climbed the stairs to the stage, received her diploma, and turned to wave at Nanny, who stood right up front, snapping one picture after another.

That night, the two of them sat in their living room, sipping hot chocolates. It was an unusually chilly May evening, and it had seemed like the perfect way to end their special day. Their home together was due in part to some of the money Lily had received as one of the triplets, or Flower Girls, as they were called at the hospital. Nanny had insisted on contributing half of the asking price, and the rest of the money had been reinvested.

"Have I told you how proud of you I am?"

"Only a hundred times," Lily replied. She patted Nanny's hand.

"I mean, you are only twenty years old and look at what you've accomplished. There aren't many who could have done what you've done, you know that, right?"

"Well, I thank God for all of it, God and you. I know he created me for a purpose, and God sent you to protect me and love me. Growing up was hard, but it's over now. I just want to be the person God created me to be."

"You will, darling girl, I'm sure of it. And I wish you would take time to go out with friends or on a date. I'm sure you could manage it."

"If it's meant to be I will, but that's not what's important to me right now. I need a few years on my own, without the constant pressure of the disapproving Rhodes family. And don't even try to say you shouldn't be here either. You make it possible for me to spend time on my studies and my career. You give me more comfort and love than anyone could ask for. There's plenty of time for dates and friends. God brought us together, me and you, and that will last a lifetime."

"I'm just so proud to share my last name with you. When I heard it called today and saw you walk on that stage, I wanted to jump up and down like a child. I think of you as my own daughter, you know. I have since the day they hired me to take care of you and placed you in my arms. Your tiny fingers curled around mine and my heart opened right up. I was thirty years old, and I'd given up on having a child. I knew I would never recover from losing my husband, and I was truly lost. God sent me you to help take away the awful pain of losing my Lawrence after only a few years together."

Lily knew the story and gently reminded her of the five years she and Lawrence had spent together. "I wish I could have met your Lawrence. I'm glad you've shared him with me a bit. I know I would have loved him. What if the two of you had been one of the couples who were chosen to adopt one of the triplets? Then I could have truly been your daughter."

"You are my daughter in every way that matters."

"Then can I call you Mom instead of Angel or Nanny?"

Tears formed in her eyes. "Are you sure you want to?"

"I'm positive. I've wanted to ask you for a long time. I just didn't know how."

The women stood and wrapped their arms around each other. "Mom," Lily whispered.

"This calls for a true celebration, don't you think? I believe I have a bottle of champagne that will do the trick." She almost skipped to the kitchen.

Lily didn't think there would ever be any moment in her life more special than this one. She held two glasses as

Nanny—Mom—came back and poured the bubbly wine, then waited for her to put down the bottle and handed one to her.

"To our mother-daughter relationship. May it always bring us pure happiness." She beamed.

"Yes, to us, with thanks to God." Lily clinked her glass against her mom's and smiled.

"Amen, Daughter. God is good, all the time."

Violet

The V-girls prevailed, despite the trauma of Violet finding out about her origin. Once she called in and completed the paperwork they sent her, the verification process began. She and her mom made the trip to the state offices of Texas, where she provided a copy of her birth certificate, was fingerprinted, and learned that her check would be on its way as soon as the others validated their claim. If they didn't validate within the two-year time frame, their share would pass on to her.

The only disappointment was that they wouldn't share anything additional about her sisters. She had the names of the Flower Girls from one of the articles released at their birth and knew her birth mother had worn a flowered dress.

Victoria had kept everything that was shared at their birth and gone over it with her. They couldn't give her anything more about Lily and Rose because of privacy issues, but she would continue to research the story until she knew more.

When the check came and she opened it up, she sat on the kitchen chair and showed it to her mom. It was made out to Violet Grace Taylor in the amount of one million, seven hundred thousand and seventy-nine dollars.

"Do you realize what this means, Mom? We're millionaires!" Violet grabbed her mom and danced her around the kitchen table. "I can pay for my own college and get a car so I can drive back to see you. Or maybe we should get you a new car and I can take yours. You know how crazy college kids can be. Wouldn't want a new car sitting there for someone to ruin or steal. Or maybe you should move closer to downtown, and after the first year in the dorm I could live there with you."

"Slow down, little girl. You realize there will be taxes due on this money, and you should probably invest at least some of it, don't you think? You already have a substantial scholarship for college, and I have saved enough over the years for the rest. Get yourself a new car if you like, but let's bank the rest. You'll be in the dorm at Rice for the first year, anyway. No need to jump into anything right now. Next year, we can start looking at houses downtown if you want to relocate closer to college so you can save money by living at home. Who knows? By then maybe some guy will sweep you off your feet and want you to move in with him."

"Don't be silly, it's going to take one special man to sweep either of us off her feet and think they're going to separate the V-girls."

"You're right about that. Anyway, I should be able to sell this house and have plenty for a down payment."

"Sounds like a great plan, Mom. I'm in no hurry to use up the money. But it sure feels good to know that my college costs won't be a burden for you."

"Violet, you couldn't be a burden to me no matter how hard you tried."

They hugged tightly and sat back down at the table. Violet picked up the check. "I wonder if Lily and Rose got their checks today. If I don't get contacted in the next two years, it will mean they both validated their claims. At that point, at least I'll know they're alive."

Violet enjoyed her first year at Rice University, completing most of her required classes and preparing to move out of the dorm the following year and into a new home for the V-girls.

Being a college student made her focus on what she liked, and she found she was really good at writing poetry and stories. When her instructor submitted one of her short stories and a poem she had written in class for a contest, she won a weekend at the Houston Art Institute to meet authors and other students who were interested in writing and speaking.

When she agreed to participate in a poetry reading, she found reading her poetry aloud added another dimension to her writing. Her poem titled "The Dragon" had the entire room so mesmerized you could have heard the dragon's breath. The applause that followed encouraged her. She knew without a doubt that she had found her career path.

Victoria was proud of her, and they talked for hours her first night home for summer break.

"Mom, you just can't imagine how fun it was at the Art Institute and how good it felt to be with people who understood me and liked my writing. It really helped me in my decision to move toward a degree in literature."

"I hope you'll read me some of your poetry. I'm sure it will be amazing. I've been cleaning out the basement and getting rid of stuff I don't need or haven't used, and I put all of your stuff on one side so you can determine what you want to keep and what to give or throw away. I've already talked to a Realtor and she doesn't think we'll have any problem selling this house. She's been sending me pictures of houses downtown to consider, but I haven't looked at anything yet. I wanted to wait so we could do it together."

"Let's make blueberry pancakes and bacon in the morning, then look through the pictures they sent you. I'm so excited to find a house together."

"I have so much to tell you about. A new book I'm reading, a new television series I think you'll love, and hey, let's get a makeover this summer."

Violet wondered why her mom was talking so fast. "Any new men in your life or hot dates I should know about?"

The color rose a bit in her mom's cheeks. "Don't be silly. You know I don't have time for that with work and all. Now, tell me about you. I bet you've met plenty of smart, attractive men at that college of yours. I want to hear all about it."

The summer flew by so fast Violet felt like it had only been days instead of months. After weeks of viewing houses, they walked into a beautiful cottage-style home in the outskirts of Houston, only minutes from Rice University. They checked out the main-floor master bedroom, with a beautiful bath and walk-in closet, and the two bedrooms upstairs with a large bathroom.

"There's plenty of room for a desk and chair between the dining area and living room where we can have a computer and such. Come on, let's go look again." Violet grabbed her mother's arm and almost dragged her up the stairs.

Violet couldn't believe how excited her mom was. She loved seeing her like this. And she had noticed the same enthusiasm in the phone calls she had in the evenings. Was that a bit of romance she felt in the air? Well, good for her. She deserved to be happy.

"I love it. It's perfect. Let's buy it."

They closed on the house two weeks later, and a little over a month after that, they had moved everything they wanted to keep out of the old house and into the new one. They had a blast shopping for new furniture, bedding, and appliances.

"It's perfect." Mom stepped back, admiring the sign she'd just hung over the door coming into the kitchen from the garage. It said *The V-Girls live here* with their names underneath. "I'm so glad you'll be here instead of the dorm this year. Now there's only one thing left to do before your classes start. We need to get a manicure."

"I agree." She walked over and hugged her mom. "I'll call first thing tomorrow."

Rose

When Rose received her check after validating that she was one of the triplets, she bought a sassy, bright-blue MINI

Cooper with white stripes. Her parents helped her invest the rest of the money, insisting that her college fund more than covered everything she would need for her education at U of H. They had all come to grips with the details of the first month of her life and decided it shouldn't interfere with everything that had happened since. They were family, and they always would be. The biggest disappointment was finding out the state could not provide information or set up a meeting with her two sisters.

Still, Rose kept the two names she had learned close to her heart. Someday, some way, she would find her sisters, Lily and Violet.

Her first two years of college went well. Rose found she had a knack for creating unique hair designs for her friends, and once her first year of basics was done, she gravitated toward design and fashion. When one of her friends asked her to create a new style for her somewhat-famous cousin, the results were amazing. Before she knew it, she was being consulted by countless women wanting makeovers.

At the end of her second year of college, she decided to finish her education at a renowned beauty school. She found a cute little shop near the school, with living quarters above, and used some of the money she had invested to purchase it. She had the plumbing modernized and added two unique beauty stations. She designed the interior herself, using only black-and-white decor, with gold fixtures and a few touches of hot-pink roses. Rose's Unique Designs was going to be a one-of-a-kind salon. She had people requesting appointments before it was even finished.

Rose's life was hectic while she attended beauty school from early morning to early afternoon, took an hour break, and scheduled appointments at the salon between one o'clock and six o'clock, taking only limited appointments for now. She insisted on her mother being her first appointment. That led to all of her mom's friends wanting appointments for makeovers, and her little salon showed signs of flourishing right from the start.

Both of her parents wanted nothing more than to see her happy, and her dad was not to be outdone. He created a computer system in the back room of her salon, with a portable module she could take with her. Rose was able to keep track of appointments, supplies, and finances, and have it at her fingertips anytime, anywhere. She had a large screen where customers could view themselves with different hairstyles and makeup before they decided what kind of look they preferred. Rose wanted her customers to have fun while finding a unique look that fit their lifestyle. Her goal was to ensure that every person who left her salon shared the excitement with the women in their circles.

The Years Fly By

At the end of beauty school, Rose was ready to put her energies into her salon full-time. She planned a grand opening and posted her hours on the door. She already had enough appointments to keep her busy for weeks, and one of her first appointments after the grand opening was Joslynn, her instructor from beauty school.

"This is really special, and I love that you used Rose in the name of the salon. There'll be no doubt as to who's creating these makeovers. And believe me, you will be noticed."

"Thanks, Joslynn. I know you don't promote your graduates unless they are seriously good, so I am truly honored that you came here. Now, let's get started. Tell me a little bit about what you are hoping for, colors you lean toward, your hair type, and styles you like. I have several books here of hairstyles and makeup, and a photo book of styles I've completed."

Two hours later, Joslynn looked in a mirror at what Rose had created. "My baby-fine hair looks thick, and the underlying layers are really nice in the back. As for the makeup line you used, you have to give me the information to order it."

"I'm so glad you like it. It really suits your complexion. And I love how that little bit of color on your eyebrows brings a bit of mystery to your overall look. I sell this line of makeup, so you can buy it right here anytime. If you want to purchase it today, I can take twenty-five percent off."

"Well, fix me up, young lady. I can't wait to show my friends. You better get ready, because I see a lot of business coming your way. You really are exceptional. You might want to consider adding someone who is good at nails, and eventually someone who can do shampoos and color for you. You need to spend your time on the design process and final touches. I'm telling you, this salon is going to be a hot spot for years to come. I know I'll be a regular customer."

After Joslynn left, Rose sat down and looked around her. This was her world, and she loved every second of it. She had given up dating and having a serious relationship, but she had accomplished so much. There was plenty of time for that. She might have started her life a little shakily, but no one would stop her now. She sent up a little prayer to the mamas in her life . . . the one who was determined to give her life and the one who would always be there for her now. She was a very lucky girl indeed.

But she still wanted to find her sisters. She looked expectantly at every Lily or Violet who made an appointment at the salon.

The Years Fly By

Detective Baxter

After Dan was finally allowed to go home from the hospital, he thought he would work hard on his recovery for a few months and then get back to his job. Donna supported and encouraged him, and they worked well together when facing something difficult. That was part of what brought them together. Still, he never dreamed every little thing would take so long to strengthen. Donna assisted him when she could, but the healing was something only his body could regulate.

The doctors, nurses, and therapists declared him a miracle and were amazed with his efforts to slowly bring his muscles and bones together again, but slowly wasn't what he wanted to hear. It was like waving a red flag in front of a bull, and it made him work even harder.

CHAPTER 6

A Triplet Reunion?

Lily

"Congratulations to Lily Flora Martino, of Martino Architectural Designs, the 2025 New Architect of the Year."

Applause filled the auditorium as Lily went up to receive her plaque. She shook hands with the announcer and waited for the applause to die down.

"Thank you all for honoring me. Starting this company fulfilled a giant dream of mine, and working with all of you has been an unbelievable experience. I believe that all of you deserve this sign of accomplishment. Thank you for the ideas and hard work that went into building one of the finest skyscrapers in Houston. I pray that we have many more years of working together. And I have to add a very special thank-you to my mom, Angel Martino. Without her help with the million and one details that came up during this project, I'm not sure we would have been this successful. I love you, Mom."

She headed toward her mom at their table and gave her a hug before she sat next to her, letting a photographer take a photo of the two of them. The photographer smiled, and Lily saw the name Violet on the large Press ID that hung around her neck.

Violet, like my sister.

In a flash, the woman moved on to the next table. Lily tried to see where she had gone, but friends and colleagues were flooding around their table to congratulate her.

Violet

During her last year in college, Violet let a friend talk her into taking a photography class, and she discovered she had a great eye for newsworthy pictures. Every now and then, she took photos when she was following something for the magazine where she worked. Writing was still her forte, but photography was fun too, and she didn't mind combining them when an opportunity arose.

At the last minute, her boss had sent her to take some pictures at an award ceremony and to follow up with an interview. The reporter originally scheduled to follow the story had an emergency in his family.

To her surprise, the woman who won the Architect of the Year award was introduced as Lily Flora Martino. Could that be one of her sisters? Oddly, she felt like it might be. They had to be about the same age. She would get the opportunity to find out when she interviewed her.

The woman was beautiful, with long, wavy blond hair, green eyes, and a flawless complexion. No one would have guessed they were sisters. Her own strawberry-blond hair got plenty of compliments, but her makeup was almost nonexistent. Maybe she and her mom really needed that makeover they had talked about years ago. It was very expensive, so they had settled with manicures, but she'd spend some of her invested money if she needed to.

She wasn't usually shy, but that woman, the architect of the year, was intimidating. It would be much easier to meet with her if Violet felt a little more pulled together. She could hardly wait to get home and share what she'd learned with her mom.

"Mom, you won't believe this. But I think I saw one of my sisters today. I had to cover an awards program for my magazine, and I took the picture of the woman named architect of the year. Her name is Lily Flora Martino, and she has to be about my age."

"My goodness! Are you going to try to contact her?"

"I'm supposed to follow up with an interview for the article in our magazine."

"Will you tell her who you are?"

"If she has remembered my name like I have hers, it might come out naturally. I don't know, maybe the others haven't wanted to know me like I have them. But before I interview her for the article, I'm going to make us appointments for makeovers."

The next morning, Violet called Rose's Unique Designs to see if there was any way she and her mom could get in. She was waiting for the receptionist to check when her mom walked into the kitchen. Muting her phone, Violet started to say good morning when the receptionist came back on the line. She put her phone on speaker so her mom could hear too.

"We have a block of time next Tuesday that should cover both of you. Do you want me to put your name down for that?"

Violet looked at her mom for confirmation. "Yes, that's wonderful. Thank you so much." She gave the receptionist their information, then hung up.

"Woo-hoo! We got a makeover appointment for next week. Thank you, Jesus!"

She called Martino Architectural Designs as soon as she got to work. "Hello, my name is Violet Taylor from *Business Daily* magazine. I'd like to schedule an interview with Lily Flora Martino and possibly feature her in our magazine. I took a couple of photos at the award ceremony last night and would love to write an article to go with them. Could I make an appointment to see her?"

"I will speak with Ms. Martino and see if she would be willing to see you." Lily's receptionist was polite and efficient. "I might be able to fit that into her schedule next week, as the project she is currently working on is concluding early. Please give me your information and I'll call you back."

"Thank you very much." Violet wondered if this beautiful woman, who had just won architect of the year, would be willing to meet with her.

She developed her photos, happy with the way they had turned out. The one of Lily and her mom was really special, as it showed how proud this mama was of her daughter.

As Violet left the developing room, her phone rang.

"I'm returning your call from this morning. Ms. Martino can see you at two o'clock next Wednesday. Does that work for you?"

"Yes. Thank you. Can you give me directions to her office?" Violet hoped her voice didn't sound as nervous as she felt. Her hands shook as she wrote down the directions.

"Don't get your hopes up," she told herself as she hung up. But it was too late. Her hopes were soaring.

Rose

Rose's salon became *the* place to go in Houston. People begged for appointments and Rose had to hire a couple more girls in addition to the ones she already had. Appointments were being scheduled months out, and she knew first-timers would go to another salon rather than wait if she didn't get help.

She'd met Tiana and Lisa at beauty school and loved the effort they put into designing nails. Their designs were top of the line, and they were excited to add their skills to Rose's salon.

She also hired two girls who were color geniuses, according to Joslynn. Aleesha was tall and thin with the most beautiful black skin Rose had ever seen, while Sally was short and blond and a bundle of energy. They had gone through beauty school together and wanted to open a salon but didn't have the capital. They were happy to team up with Rose, whom they had heard nothing but praise for.

A Triplet Reunion?

Rose purchased the building next to hers, which had been for sale for ages. She got it for a song, and her dad called in favors from a construction company he knew. In no time, Rose's Unique Designs more than doubled. All five girls loved what they did. They were so successful they were advertised in *Cover Girl* and other magazines.

When Rose saw the name Lily M. on the appointment calendar, she wondered for a second about her sister. But she didn't know her last name, so she didn't give it another thought.

When Lily came into the salon, Rose liked her immediately. Her natural beauty made it fun to give her a style that would enhance it even more but also give her a casual look that was fun and a little sassy. By the end of the appointment, the girls were fast friends.

A month later, when Rose saw the names Violet and Victoria Taylor on her schedule, her excitement rose again. The day they came in, she introduced herself by her full name as she sat at her desk. "Hello, ladies. I am Rose Maria Cortez, and I will be creating a unique design for each of you. Please tell me a little bit about what you are looking for, any hair color or style you're thinking about, and anything else I should know about you."

The younger woman gasped and whispered something to the older one, who nodded. "I'm Violet Grace Taylor. I'm one of the Texas Flower Girls. Does that mean anything to you?"

"Violet?" Rose stood and came around her desk. Violet met her halfway. Their hug was awkward, but emotion radiated between them. "I have wondered since you made the appointment if it was really you. Every time someone named Violet or Lily calls in for an appointment, I wonder if it could be one of my sisters. But this time felt different, and I prayed I would be right." She sat back down. "I'm just stunned."

Violet sat too. "I felt the same way a week or so ago when I covered an awards program for my magazine. When Lily Flora Martino walked up to the stage to accept her Architect of the Year award, I just stood there, gaping. I managed to get a quick picture of her and her mom before I left, then I followed up with an interview, which is scheduled for tomorrow. I'm so hoping it's her."

"Oh, my gosh, I know her. She was in a month ago for a makeover."

"No way! I wanted to come here for a makeover so I would feel confident enough to meet with her because she's so beautiful. And you're beautiful too. I can't believe I may have found both of you."

"After I give both of you the unique makeover you signed up for, we have to plan time to get together." She turned to Violet's mother. "I'm sorry. You must be Victoria."

"Yes, I am. I know what this means for both of you. But I'm also really excited about this makeover."

"Then let's get started. You can go first while Violet looks through a couple of books I have, to think about the kind of look she wants."

Rose noticed that Violet watched and listened while her mother shared likes, dislikes, colors, and styles. She shook her head at the miracle she had prayed for so often. Her head spun with thoughts of all three of them getting together and sharing the rest of their lives. But she knew she was getting ahead of herself. She pulled her attention back to Victoria.

Usually by the time she got home, Rose was exhausted. Her mom would have something waiting for her to warm up, along with a small glass of their favorite Riesling wine. Tonight, Rose almost ran into the house. "Mom!" she yelled when she didn't see her in the kitchen.

Mom came from their living room at a jog. "What's wrong?"

"Nothing. I found one of my sisters today, and I might know where the other one is. I can't believe it." She sat on one of the stools and picked up the glass of wine from the counter.

"What?" Her mom picked up the other glass of wine and sat beside her.

"Remember I told you that Victoria and Violet Taylor made appointments at the salon?"

"Of course. And I told you not to get your hopes up."

"Well, they came in today, and Violet is my sister. I designed a makeover for her and her mom. They both have the most beautiful strawberry-blond hair I've ever seen. Violet is covering Lily for a magazine article and thinks she's our other sister. I met her when she came in for a makeover, but I wasn't sure it was her. It has to be, though, because she mentioned that she was an architect, and Violet was covering an award ceremony for Architect of the Year."

"Oh, Rose, that's wonderful! Do you think you'll all try to get together?"

"I hope so. Lily and I really hit it off, and she made a follow-up appointment. At the very least, she'll be in for that and I can share what I know. And Violet is so sweet. I really like her too. She's meeting Lily tomorrow to interview her for the magazine she works for. We exchanged numbers and Violet is going to call me as soon as it's over."

"I am so happy for you, honey. And you need to know that we would welcome two more daughters into our family. Do you think they might look at us as another set of parents?

I mean, I assume they had good families and have their own parents, but I hope they will consider all of us part of their family too."

"I don't know what this might mean for the Flower Girls. But there is one other question I need to have answered. What happened to our mother and father?"

Detective Baxter

Eventually Dan convinced his therapists and his boss that he was ready to get back to work. No one had been able to follow up on the case of the triplets because he had all the info in his head. And while his head was one of the few things that had not been physically damaged in the crash, the trauma and resulting coma had done a number on even that.

When he finally got back into his office, he had to keep it part-time at first. His body would not be pushed any faster, and even that much effort exhausted him. He cursed the accident that had made him less than he had been, at least temporarily.

CHAPTER 7

Triplets and Sisters

Lily

Lily woke up and jumped out of bed. Today was the day she would meet Violet Taylor of *Business Daily* magazine. Could she be one of the Flower Girl triplets? Did she already know? Lily was dressed and ready to go when she heard her mom calling from her bedroom.

"Do you want breakfast today, Lily?"

"Nope. I need to get to the office early. I have to find out if Violet Taylor is one of the Flower Girls." She walked down the hall to her mom's room. "What do you think? Is this dress okay?"

"Oh, honey, you always look beautiful, no matter what you wear. Now, come give me a hug. Want an English muffin to take with you? I can have it ready for you in a jiffy."

"I don't think so. I'm so jittery I would probably throw up if I ate something. Why don't we meet for lunch afterward and I can tell you all about my sister!"

Violet

Violet stood in the lobby of a large commercial building sandwiched between two other buildings in downtown Houston. She entered the elevator and hit the button for the eighth floor. On the way up, she took out her compact and looked at the strawberry-blond waves that just touched her shoulders and the makeup that highlighted her brows and lips. Rose had managed to create a new look while keeping the changes minimal. She snapped the compact closed and returned it to her purse just as the elevator dinged.

Down the hall she located the door marked Martino Architectural Designs, went in, and approached the receptionist. "Hello. I'm Violet Taylor from *Business Daily* magazine."

"Ms. Martino will be with you in a few minutes. Follow me." She stood and led Violet to a large room with a conference table and chairs and an impressive view of the city. "Can I get you something to drink? Water? Soda?"

"A bottle of water would be perfect. Thank you."

She admired the view for a moment, then took a seat.

The receptionist returned with the water. "Ms. Martino will be with you shortly."

As she gazed out the window, Violet recalled the story she had heard from her mom about what had happened the day of her birth. The details were sketchy, and she thought she'd like to visit the detective who had worked on the case all those years ago. But right now, she wanted to meet her sister. Would she be cool and reserved? Warm and interested in pursuing a relationship?

Before her thoughts went any further, footsteps came down the hall. The woman who walked in was so beautiful, it was hard not to be overwhelmed.

"Hello. I'm Lily Flora Martino. You must be Violet Taylor from *Business Daily*. I think I saw you at the award ceremony."

"Yes. It's good to meet you." Violet came around the table to shake hands with her. "I got some great photos that night that I'd love to share with you, and I'm hoping you'll allow me to write an article to go with them."

"I would be honored to answer questions about my job and the award, and I'd love to see your photos, but first I have a question for you. Are you one of three triplets born in Texas and nicknamed the Flower Girls?"

"Yes! Yes, I am." Violet threw her arms around Lily, shaking with emotion. Lily's arms wrapped around her in return. "I had almost given up on ever finding you, but when I heard your name announced at the award program, I just knew it was you. It was a fluke that I was even covering that event, so I felt it had to be a sign. You know, a God thing."

She pulled Lily over to the chairs around the conference table but did not let go of her hand.

"I know exactly what you mean. I have prayed and prayed that I would find my sisters. Your names have been whirling around in my head for years, ever since I got the validation paperwork. Whenever I heard the name Violet or Rose, I caught my breath."

"It's been the same for me. All my life I felt like something was missing. I was raised by a single mom, and her husband divorced her right after I arrived. But she is the greatest mom ever, and I hope you can meet her one day. She's going to be over the moon about having another daughter. That is, if you want to. We'll understand if you don't. You probably have great parents too. It was obvious from your pictures that your mom loves you very much."

"That's a story for another time. I'm glad you didn't give up when you heard my name. I wasn't as lucky as you. My parents only adopted me for the publicity that would help their careers. They hired a nanny, who took care of me and shared my room right from the start. She's the best, and now we share a house together. She's my mom in every sense of the word, so I changed my last name to match hers. I know she'll want to meet you." She reached out a hand and touched Violet's hair. "You're so pretty."

"Well, you are absolutely beautiful. And there's something else I have to tell you. I believe I know where our third triplet is. I met her, and you did too. You just didn't know it was her. It's Rose, from Rose's Unique Designs."

"No way! I wondered if she was my sister. But there was no way to broach the subject. Then we got all caught up in the makeover and I forgot about it. We really hit it off and I made another appointment. Are you sure she's our sister?"

"No doubt about it. And she is hoping that we are the Flower Girl triplets and can finally be real sisters. We still have so much of life to share."

"How do we do it—get together, I mean? I just finished a project and planned to take this weekend off work. Maybe we could do a night together. A friend of mine owns the ZaZa Hotel near here. I could probably get us a suite or something."

"That sounds amazing. Do you have the time to give Rose a call with me right now? She'll be dying to know what came out of our meeting."

"Of course. Let me tell my receptionist to cancel my next appointment." She left the room briefly, then came back and closed the door. "Okay. Let's do it."

Violet pulled out her phone, dialed, and put it on speaker so they could both hear. Within seconds, a businesslike voice answered.

"This is Rose at Rose's Unique Designs. How can I help you?"

"Rose, it's Violet. I'm at my interview with Lily, and I was right. She is the third triplet—our sister!"

Rose

"What did you say?" Rose's voice and hands shook.

"It's true. Lily's right here with me."

"Hi, Rose. It's Lily. And it's true. I am one of the Texas Flower Girls."

Rose took a deep breath. "Do you guys want to get together and meet somewhere?"

"I'm going to see if a friend of mine can pull some strings and get us rooms at the ZaZa Hotel Friday night," Lily offered. "Would you be able to make that?"

"Just tell me what time and I'll be there."

"If that doesn't work for any reason, we can meet at my house," Violet added. "My mom would be thrilled."

"I'm pretty sure I can make it happen," Lily said. "Let's say seven o'clock in the hotel lobby. I don't believe I really have two sisters . . . Violet and Rose. Do you realize we all have flower names?"

"Yeah, I noticed that when I read the validation papers," Rose said. "I guess our biological mom liked flowers. I've been wanting to talk to the detective who was assigned our case, but now maybe we can do it together. Violet and Lily, my beautiful sisters. It seems so surreal."

"I'm pretty sure we're all feeling a bit stunned," Violet said. "I can't wait until we're together Friday night."

After an awkward moment, they said their goodbyes. Rose was sure it was the most important conversation she'd ever have in her life. She sat staring into space for several moments, thankful the only clients in the shop were in the next room getting manicures.

Friday was a very busy day for Rose, and it wasn't until early afternoon that she could take a break. She sat in the break room, having a cold soda and daydreaming. "I have two sisters, and I'm going to meet them in a couple of hours," she whispered. "Yikes! I have to get ready." She checked the names on the computer and confirmed that the rest of the day's appointments were all with repeat clients for touch-ups or manicure customers.

She rushed out into the salon. "Aleesha, can you handle the rest of the appointments this afternoon?" She nodded, her smooth forehead furrowed with confusion. "And can you clear my schedule for tomorrow? If anyone wants to wait to see me specifically, ask them to reschedule."

"Are you okay? You look a little pale."

"I'm better than okay. But I have to run a couple of errands. I'll fill you in on Monday. Thank you so much. You know I wouldn't do this if it wasn't important." She gave Aleesha a quick hug, then hugged Sally as she came in from the back room with the color for their next client. Then she grabbed her purse from her office and rushed out the back door.

Detective Baxter

Once Baxter got back to a full-time work schedule, he listened again to the recording on the phone that had miraculously survived the accident. He documented everything from the recording, shared it with his boss, and got the paperwork for the trip to the Mexican border within days.

Knowing approximately where the lady who saved Clara had traveled, he crossed into Mexico, parked his car just inside the row of pines, and found the trail she had mentioned. The hard-packed dirt was barely visible.

He figured out the general area where the women had been kept, then found the charred remains of a small building among the weeds that came to above his knees. The place was indeed in the middle of nowhere, but in spite of years of overgrowth, he located the burnt-out garage and the metal frame of a vehicle. Could this be what was left of the mysterious black Jaguar?

He walked around to where the back of the building would have been, noticing the bushes where the wagon that had carried Clara must have been stashed by the unknown woman. As he stood there trying to look through the heavy brush and trees, he started to visualize how everything could have unfolded.

Following a small path in the woods, he found the road where the vehicle had waited for them, within a few feet of where his own car stood. It was a miracle they had managed to escape.

His next stop was the Mexican police station to find out what had happened to destroy the buildings and who had been responsible. He hoped someone there would be honest with him. It was a shot in the dark. The men had likely all scattered by now.

Baxter got no information about who had started the fire. It had been listed as an act of nature.

"Seriously?"

"That's what I said." The police officer stared at him.

"What about the car in the garage? Was it a Jaguar?"

"It could have been any kind of vehicle. No need to waste time tracing it. There were no signs of human remains or foul play. It all happened a long time ago. Why the interest now?"

"We're following up on a cold case and wanted to rule out anything that might have connected it to Mexico. Thanks for your help."

He left, knowing that it *had* been connected to something here, but he wasn't likely to get any help to prove it.

On his way back to his precinct, he stopped at the fight club to see if Mr. Macho Maxwell had made it out of that Mexican hellhole alive.

When he got to the club, he hit another road block. The club had been closed—for a while, by the look of things. He walked around the outside of the empty building, hoping for some sign of the woman he knew had been kidnapped and tortured. The only thing he came across was a nest of mice.

Back at the station, he realized the case might stay closed, in spite of all that he had learned about Clara. Still, he was determined to document everything he knew.

The real miracle in the whole story was the fact that the two women had survived at all. The woman who had persevered to save an innocent kidnapping victim and the mama who was determined to save her babies at all costs.

CHAPTER 8

The Flower Girls, Reunited

Lily

The lobby at the ZaZa Hotel was busy, and the elegance took Lily's breath away. She arrived early and spoke with her friend Jody about their rooms. They had met years ago at college but still kept in touch. They hugged each other tightly.

"I hope this isn't a problem."

"For you, my friend, it's never a problem. And you're in luck tonight. Our penthouse is available, and I'm happy to let you use it."

"How much?"

"Girl, did you ever let me pay you for the hours of tutoring you gave me in college? The times you had to talk me off the ledge over one of the guys I fell for? Or the hours I consulted with you about building this hotel? It's an honor to pay you back in some small way. Here are your keys, and my staff is at your service. Just ring us and your wish will be granted."

The hug that followed was even tighter than the first. "Thank you, my friend. Do you remember me telling you about the triplet story?" Jody nodded. "I'm meeting them here tonight. It will be the first time we have been together since the month we spent in the Texas hospital as newborns. Against all odds, we found each other."

"Are you kidding?"

"Nope. Here's one of them now."

Violet came in the door, pulling a dark purple roller bag. As Lily waved her over, the door swished open and another woman entered, also pulling a bag. When Violet grabbed her hand and pointed toward Lily, she knew it had to be Rose. She met them halfway, and the three girls wrapped their arms around one another.

"I can't believe we're together," Lily said. "This is such a dream come true. Come meet my friend Jody. She runs this hotel and has a special treat for us." She took the women to her friend. "Jody, these are my sisters, Violet and Rose. Sisters, this is my dear friend Jody."

"I'm so happy to meet you. I've been trying to get Lily to stay here for years."

"It's good to meet you," Rose said, "and even better to be here with these two. Can we split the cost of the room three ways?"

"Oh, honey, the room's on me. I owe this girl more than she knows." She touched one of Rose's dark, shiny curls. "I knew Lily was gorgeous, but the three of you together put even that word to shame." A customer waved at her. "I've got to go. You girls have fun, and I'll see you all later." She hurried off.

"This place is amazing," Violet whispered.

"Let's check out our rooms." Lily handed each of the girls a key card and they headed to the elevators.

A bellman took their bags and followed them. When Lily pushed the button for the penthouse suite, Violet gasped. "You've got to be kidding."

"Nope. It's good to know people in high places, right?"

Lily led them off the elevator and headed toward the double doors marked *Penthouse* in gold letters.

"I can hardly believe this is happening." Lily gave Rose another hug.

They entered the most splendid room Lily had ever seen. A bottle of wine and three crystal glasses sat on an ornate glass table in the entryway. A note said simply, *Enjoy!*

The bellman set down their bags, refusing the tip Lily tried to slip into his hand. "Enjoy your stay, ladies." He tipped his hat at them and left.

The main room had luxurious sofas and chairs surrounding a long, low, ornate glass table. A three-foot-tall gift basket sat on it. Through the cellophane holding it together, Lily saw snacks of every variety. The kitchen encompassed one side of the room, with an open doorway to a powder room a little farther down. The other side of the room had four open doors. Three led to bedrooms and the fourth gave a peak at a huge free standing bathtub.

Rose drifted to the first room, and Lily followed, looking over her shoulder. "This pink bedroom looks amazing! I love pink. And look at the beautiful vase of hot pink roses."

"Pretty sure that room is meant for you." Lily smiled.

Violet

Violet went on to the next room. "Look at the violets. This has to be mine." She turned to look at Lily, who smiled. "You knew, didn't you?"

"I wasn't sure what to expect, but Jody knew all of your names, so I'm not surprised. And look . . . mine is mostly white with hints of aquamarine, which she knows I like. And the lilies are beautiful." She wheeled her bag inside.

They all had small bathrooms with showers in their rooms, but the bathroom with the big tub called to her. Violet left her bag in her room and went to look at it again.

The tub took up most of the room, with seats molded into each corner and jets all around. It was more like a hot tub than a bathtub. A huge pile of oversized bath towels and washcloths were piled on a bench nearby, and a shelf in the corner held a variety of bath soaps, oils, salts, and creams. It was a dream.

"Come on, girls," Lily called, "we need to have a toast."

Violet went to the living room and sat on one of the plush sofas, patting the space beside her. Rose joined her while Lily opened the bottle of wine and handed glasses to her sisters. She poured carefully, including a glass for herself.

"Here's to us, the Flower Girls of Texas." Violet raised her glass, the other girls clinked their glasses to it, and all three took their first sip of the delightful wine.

"Can you believe people gave us all that money?" Violet asked.

"Right?" Rose agreed. "I mean, I hated finding out that my mom and dad weren't biological, but I got over it. They've been the best parents any child could ask for. I used some of my money to start the salon, but they suggested I invest the rest, and I know they are always there for me. They're eager to meet both of you."

Lily swallowed a sip. "You were lucky, Rose. My family was less than ideal. They let me know right from the start that I wasn't part of the family. But God sent me a guardian angel. They hired a nanny to look after me, and she became the mother I never had."

"My mom has been amazing," Violet said. "But her husband divorced her right after they got me, so I never knew him. We are the V-girls, Victoria and Violet. The funny thing is, her hair and eyes are the same color as mine, so no one ever guesses that I'm adopted. I feel lucky to be hers. And she can't wait to meet you both."

Lily put down her glass, laced her fingers together, and looked at Violet and Rose. "Do either of you know anything about our biological mother and father or what happened? All I know is that we were born at a little hospital in Del Rio, Texas, just this side of the Mexican border, and a detective was assigned our case."

Rose set down her glass. "My parents told me that a Detective Baxter was assigned the case and that our mother was badly abused before she got to the hospital. I think that means they considered her death a homicide. Somehow she got to the hospital, and because she wouldn't give up, we all lived." A tear made its way down Rose's cheek.

All three girls hugged and cried together.

Finally, Violet pushed back. "I don't know if it will do any good, but I plan to go to that hospital and see if anyone can tell us anything. And if this Detective Baxter is still alive, I'll talk to him too. Someone has to know more than we do."

Rose brushed away her tears. "I'm with you."

Lily threw her hand into the middle of them, palm down. "Count me in too. Three voices are stronger than one."

Two more hands slapped on top of hers.

"Now, what's for dinner?" Violet asked. "I'm starving."

The door chimed and she went to answer, her sisters looking over her shoulders. When the door opened, in came three hotel waiters. One told them to take a seat at the table outside the kitchen.

The servers placed fancy china, silverware, and condiments in front of them, then wheeled over a cart that held three chafing dishes. After placing them on the table, they unlidded each with a flare. One had beef tenderloin with tiny potatoes, carrots, and onions. The next had a chicken breast in a buttery lemon sauce, and the last one had lobster tails around a bowl of melted butter.

The hotel staff smiled and bowed, and the head waiter told the girls to ring room service when they were finished.

When the door closed, the girls burst into laughter.

By the end of the meal, all three were stuffed. They called room service, and within minutes the staff members had loaded their cart and were out the door.

Rose

Rose brushed imaginary crumbs off her jeans. "Well, I think it's past time for pajamas. I'm about to burst the seams of these jeans." She headed for her room, followed by her sisters.

A few minutes later, all three returned to the luxurious sofas to nibble on the shortbread cookies with raspberry centers that the staff had left on the table.

"I'd be big as a barn if I ate like this all the time." Rose giggled. "No makeover would hide that."

"The fact that it's not the norm is what makes it taste so good," Lily said. "Besides, none of us could ever be called chubby, now, could we?" Rose and Lily laughed as they watched Violet try to pinch the skin on her arm, but it stayed firmly in place.

"I'd say we all have a healthy metabolism. I wonder where that came from," Lily said in a solemn tone. "We don't even know if we have the same father. We're all so different, other than our slender build."

Violet frowned. "We're triplets. Wouldn't that mean we have the same father?"

"Not necessarily. Lily's right." Rose put her feet up on the ottoman. "Fraternal multiples could have different dads. I looked it up."

Not liking the atmosphere of sadness that had crept into the room, Rose leaned toward her sisters. "Let's take turns telling each other about ourselves."

Dawn was shining through the window before the girls stopped talking. Grabbing blankets from their rooms, they all agreed to sleep on the couches. They couldn't bear the thought of separating so soon.

When they awoke, breakfast sat on the table waiting for them: bacon and fluffy scrambled eggs in a large ceramic warming dish, flaky croissants, and fresh berries with whipped cream. On the counter, an electric pot of steaming coffee wafted a scent that got them stirring.

Rose shuffled to the pot and poured three steaming cups. "Anyone want cream or sugar?"

The other girls shook their heads, yawning, and sniffing deeply as they slipped into chairs and picked up their cups.

"You can't beat this." Violet took a sip. "Lily, is this really the first time you've stayed here?"

"Yep."

Rose sighed. "I'd come as often as I could. I thought my salon was plush, but it's nothing compared to this."

"Your salon is perfect," Lily said. "I'm just glad I got to experience this with the two of you. Maybe this will be our first tradition . . . a night away from home with the sisters. I don't know if we can afford this place every time, but we can split the cost three ways at a less luxurious place. Being together is the main thing. I'm sure Jody has less expensive suites."

Rose walked to a window that overlooked a beautiful flower garden, and Lily and Violet joined her.

"I don't care where we stay," Violet said, "as long as we're together."

Rose returned to the table. "I already feel like we've known each other forever. I can't imagine life without the two of you."

"Me too," Lily said. "Your names have rolled around in my brain almost constantly for the last six years."

"Same for me," Violet said. "When I took pictures of you and your mom, Lily, I felt close to you right away."

"I'm glad you followed up," Lily said. "Now none of us has to wonder another minute. We may have missed twenty-four years of being sisters, but I'm ready to move forward as if I have always had you in my life."

"I second that." Violet high-fived Rose.

"Me too!" Lily started to high-five them but ended up wrapping an arm around each of them instead. "We are the Flower Girl triplets of Texas."

"And we stand together as one," Rose added.

Detective Baxter

When Baxter got back to the station, he sat down heavily on his chair. He still tired easily, but he knew he had been lucky to survive the accident. Still, he had hoped to solve the case of the Texas Flower Girls. All he had accomplished was discovering that the mother's first name was Clara.

"Hey, Baxter, any luck?" His boss popped his head in the doorway.

"Nothing I didn't already know. I guess the case will have to stay closed."

"Sorry to hear that." His boss leaned against the corner of his desk. "By the way, a reporter from some magazine called wanting to talk to you. Helen took the message and her number." He handed him a piece of paper with the information on it.

"Thank you, sir."

After his boss left, Baxter read the note:

Violet Taylor from *Business Daily* magazine would like to talk to you. Said she's one of the Flower Girls, if that means anything to you.

"Yes, it does!" He looked around to make sure no one had heard him. Then he picked up his phone and dialed the number for the magazine.

CHAPTER 9

Life as the Flower Girl Triplets

Lily

*L*ily worked feverishly all day on Monday, catching up on things she'd let go on Friday. Even though she was supposed to be working, she caught herself staring out the window at the Houston skyline, grinning like a Cheshire cat. Violet and Rose, *her sisters,* were coming to dinner tonight to meet her mom.

Lily imagined her mom at home hustling around like crazy, ensuring every little thing was in place. She'd have fresh flowers and good china on the table, their best salt and pepper grinders, and pretty napkins rolled around the silverware. She knew without a doubt it would look perfect. They had purchased a turkey breast, rice, multicolored carrots, and white onions, all of which had been in the crockpot when she left this morning. She would smell the fresh rosemary and garlic when she got home, and maybe the apple cake that was Nanny's mother's recipe, full of apples, pecans, and raisins.

No one would go home hungry tonight.

Violet

Violet kept her disappointment in check when she found out Detective Baxter was not at his desk. She had finished the article on the architect of the year with new insight. But she ached for more details.

She dropped the article and picture off to the editor, then thought about clearing her desk and visiting the police station. As she was about to leave, her phone rang.

"Hello. Is Miss Taylor there?"

"I'm Miss Taylor. How can I help you?"

"This is Detective Dan Baxter. I understand you're one of the Texas Flower Girls. I've been the lead detective on this case since you were born. Have you located the other two triplets?"

"I have. We'd like to meet with you to discuss the case regarding our birth mother." She tried to keep her voice calm.

"That's great. I have documented everything I know, and I'd be happy to share it with you all. We could meet at the Waldorf, near the police station. Say tomorrow around five?"

"That sounds fine. I'll let my sisters know." Violet's heart raced and her stomach felt like jelly as she hung up. Her legs were so shaky she had to sit down.

What would they find out? Would they finally know what had happened to their biological parents? She could hardly wait till tonight to tell Rose and Lily they would be meeting with the detective the next evening.

Rose

Rose worked double time on Monday, trying to fit in all the appointments she had missed on Saturday. But the smile never left her face. She had filled in her coworkers first thing this morning, and the aura in the salon was exhilarating. *I'm having dinner with my sisters tonight.* She tried to hold down the joy that wanted to rise up and spill out of her like a fountain. Her clients got an extra dose of happiness that day, and her designs were exceptional. Having sisters was a plus in so many ways.

"You look like you're about to burst with happiness," Aleesha told her after one of her appointments was completed.

"I am. I have begged my parents for sisters since I was five, and now I have two of the most beautiful, talented sisters anyone could hope for."

"Just remember, there's bad as well as good in sister relationships. I can tell you that from experience. But it sounds like you got lucky. I hope it lasts."

"We've already missed out on over twenty years of being sisters, so we have a lot to make up for. This weekend was a total blast. I expect it to get better every time we're together." Rose tidied up her area, putting everything in its proper place.

"You're probably right. I can drop off our deposit at the bank tonight if you want. I have to stop there myself anyway."

"Thanks. That will give me a little extra time to get ready for dinner with Violet, Lily, and Lily's mom."

The rest of the day flew by, and before she knew it she was on her way.

She pulled up to a pretty condo with beautiful landscaping. Before she could get out of the car, Violet parked beside her. The smile on her face mimicked the one that had been on Rose's all day. Violet gave her the biggest hug. Arm in arm, they walked up the sidewalk and Lily opened the door to welcome them.

Detective Baxter

Baxter pulled together everything he had on the case of the tortured woman who had delivered triplets. The file was thick, but he wanted the girls to know how hard he had tried to find those responsible for their mother's death.

He stopped by the library on his way home to make sure he hadn't missed anything. The first time he'd gone there, Margaret, the manager, informed him that Janice, the pregnant girl working at the library, had not lived to save her baby boy after she was shot. Her distraught husband had moved back to Rhode Island to be with family and friends.

She had promised to let the detective know if she heard anything else. He had checked back with her over the years, but the accident had kept him away for a while.

When he went inside, he saw Margaret standing behind the counter. She stepped through one of the bulletproof doors that had been installed following the tragic shooting and kidnapping.

"Hello, Detective. Long time, no see." A broad smile filled her face.

"Hello, Margaret. How have you been?"

"Just fine. Did I hear something about you being in a bad automobile crash?"

"Yeah. Took me a while to recover, but I'm back at it."

"I'm glad. I finally came up with something about those pregnant women."

"You did?"

"I tried calling your precinct, but they told me you were on leave, and then I forgot about it."

She hobbled to a door at the rear of the library, and he followed. She opened it to a cluttered mess of papers and stacks of books. She brought out a thick album. "I found two of these. One behind the counter on the floor that obviously belonged to Janice, the woman from Rhode Island, who was shot and killed. I called her husband and he took it with him. This is the other one, and it has the name Clara on the inside. I found it under one of the bookshelves near the desk when we reorganized. No telling how it ended up there." She handed it to him.

"Thank you very much. The triplets have reunited and are looking for any scrap of information they can find about their mother. I'm meeting with them tomorrow. I'm sure they'd love to have something that was hers."

"No problem, Detective." The library phone rang, and she hurried back behind the desk.

Back at home, he took a moment to leaf through the album and realized it was a journal of Clara's pregnancy. It covered her husband leaving and all she had gone through only to find out that he hadn't been who she thought he was. Even his name was obviously fictitious, so she had gone back to her maiden name. She grieved for months before she finally pulled it together.

She had documented how she had been trying for years to get pregnant and, since her husband had claimed he was sterile, had used her own eggs with donor sperm in hopes of having a child. She hadn't been successful before, but she knew she still had three eggs left under her contract. She went to her doctor and made the decision to have all three eggs fertilized and implanted, hoping at least one would result in a child to share her life with. She was elated when she found out she was pregnant, and again when her ultrasound showed triplets. She wrote about how much her precious daughters meant to her already.

Baxter choked up a bit and closed the journal. The girls would be ecstatic, but he felt less so. There was no mention of her last name, doctor's name, or anything that could help the case.

Was it possible that Maxwell had been after Janice instead of Clara? Maybe he took Clara by mistake, then saw the other girl come out of the restroom and killed her to hide it. At this point, with burnt-out, closed-down buildings and questionable information, it was impossible to verify anything. This case was a nightmare of catastrophes.

CHAPTER 10

Meeting the Family

Lily

The women chatted like they had known each other for years, and Mom looked on like a proud mother hen. Her dinner was a hit, and she walked around the table picking up empty plates and taking anything that wasn't needed back to the kitchen.

"Mom, stop waiting on us. You're here to meet the girls."

"Well, I *have* met them, and now I'm preparing the table for my special apple cake."

"If I eat one more bite of anything, I'll explode." Rose puffed out her cheeks.

"Silly girl. You're skinny, just like my Lily. Everyone has room for a little slice of heaven, right?"

"Mrs. Martino, you spoil us," Violet said. "Dinner was exceptional. And now cake? Well, I for one will force myself, if you insist."

"Thank you, sweet Violet, and yes, I insist. But please, just Angel . . . or even better, Mom. If you're Lily's sisters, you must be my daughters."

"How about Mama Martino?" Lily smiled at her. "Does that work for you?"

"Why, yes, it does. I'll go get my cake." She headed to the kitchen.

"You guys are in for a treat. The cake is a recipe from her mother. It really is like a little slice of heaven."

Her mom came back with the cake and small plates. After everyone had devoured their dessert and complimented her over and over, they took coffee into the living room, where they could relax and talk. Lily invited Mom to join them, but she opted to stay back and tidy up.

Violet

"Well, spill it, Sister. Do we have an appointment with the detective?" Rose asked.

"We do," Violet answered, sitting down next to them on the sofa. "He's meeting us tomorrow at the Waldorf. He says the case is closed at this point, but he will share everything he has discovered over the years."

"Perfect." Lily clasped her hands.

"He's coming right from work and wants to meet at five o'clock. Is that good for everyone?"

They all nodded.

"Knowing what happened to our mother won't change what we've found together, right?" Violet asked. "I feel so close to both of you, and I don't want to lose that."

The three women huddled together.

"What we have is forever, sister," Lily said. "I feel like I have been watching and waiting for you my whole life."

"We are the Flower Girls of Texas," Rose added. "Nothing's going to change that."

Rose

As Rose drove home, tears welled up in her eyes. She had wanted sisters for so long, and now she had them. She remembered a day at church, long ago, when she had badgered her mom about wanting sisters. Mom had told her to pray about it, and she did. She was disappointed when they didn't show up immediately.

Now she prayed again. "God, you know I prayed for sisters, and you knew the plan you had for us. Thank you for answering my prayers. You have blessed us beyond belief, and I pledge to you, Father, that I will never forget or take for granted what you have given us. Amen."

Detective Baxter

Baxter was nervous about meeting the women he had known as infants. He'd been so excited when he was assigned the case. But one look at the tiny babies had sobered him. This was serious business, and those little girls would depend on *him* to find answers.

Now he had to tell them what little he had discovered over the years. Despite all of the efforts he had put into solving the case, and what it had caused him personally, he felt like he had failed them.

Three women entered the hotel lobby together, and Baxter knew from his internet search they were the Flower Girls. Although he had seen how attractive they were online, seeing their beauty in person took his breath away.

"Good evening. I'm Detective Baxter. You three have to be the Flower Girls. It's been a long time since I've seen you."

One of them stepped forward. "I'm Violet Taylor. We spoke on the phone. These are my sisters, Lily Martino and Rose Cortez."

He shook hands with each of them. "I've reserved a private room so we can talk undisturbed." He led them down the hall.

After they were seated around the table, each woman gave him a brief explanation of their current life and how they had all reconnected.

"I wish I could tell you that your mother's case has been solved. Unfortunately, it hasn't. For twenty-four years, I have followed leads for this case, only to come up empty-handed. But there are a few facts I have discovered along the way."

Three nods kept him talking.

"To begin with, your mother's name was Clara."

They looked at each other, smiling at the crumb he was able to offer them.

"In the beginning, right after you were born, all we knew was that your mother had been horribly abused. She made it to the emergency room at approximately two in the morning, badly beaten, with signs of having been restrained and tortured. She asked for help to save her babies and mentioned she was carrying triplets."

The women held one another's hands.

"Immediately following your birth, she passed. There were notices on the news and in the papers asking anyone with information to come forward. Other than a couple of people who couldn't prove any kind of relationship or give information about your mother, no one came forward to claim you. Since no one offered to take on triplets, you were all adopted by different families."

Their calm looks told him they already knew those details.

"My first tip was about a man your mother was seen with in an old café the night you were born. He owned a fight club. He didn't like me asking him questions and threatened me until I left. I went back recently, and the place was boarded up and looked deserted."

The women were hanging on his every word now.

"Then I spoke with the manager of the Home Town Library, where your mother was kidnapped. The previous manager, who was also pregnant and thought to be a friend of your mom's, was shot and killed that night. The new manager claimed she couldn't provide any information about the woman who was kidnapped."

The women's wide eyes made him wonder if he shouldn't have told them about the other pregnant women. But he'd promised to tell them everything he knew that was related to the case.

"I checked with several medical offices, thinking they would have information on someone who was pregnant with triplets, but no luck. I was told over and over that there were hundreds of such offices in Houston and surrounding towns. Without a last name no one could help."

The sadness on the girls' faces made him glad he had some good news for them.

"I went back to visit the manager at the library last night, and she gave me something of your mother's." Dan pulled out the journal and saw sparks of hope flash in the sisters' eyes.

"It was found during a remodel of the library a few years ago. The other pregnant woman had one as well. I believe your mom went to the library that night to show Janice her journal so they could compare them. My theory is that Janice went back to the break room to get her journal, and the man grabbed Clara instead of Janice, knocking the journal out of her hands. When Janice came out of the breakroom, he had to shoot her because she saw him dragging Clara out. It's all speculation, but it would explain everything."

He paused to let them soak that in before continuing. "I have a bit more knowledge to share. About ten years ago, I got a call from someone who asked to remain anonymous. We met, and she told me what she knew about Clara. This woman had been in a clinic in Mexico where pregnant women were taken. It was operated as a safe house for unwed mothers until they gave birth, but the men who ran it sold the babies after they were born. If the girls weren't willing to give up their babies, they disappeared. The lady I talked to said the men who ran the place were evil."

The women gasped, and tears filled their eyes. He took a box of tissues off the counter and placed in on the table.

"She helped your mother out of the clinic and got her to the hospital where you were born, Sisters of Mercy Hospital in Del Rio, Texas. After that, she disappeared. She reached out to me now because she's dying from a complication caused by a pneumonia virus, and she believed Clara's story should be told. At least what she knew of it."

He took a deep breath before continuing.

"I have followed up with the Mexican police, but they are not fond of helping Americans. I was able to locate the site where the building they stayed in had been, but it had mysteriously burned to the ground and no one had any other information. An act of nature, they said. I think there might be a connection between Maxwell, the man who owned the fight club, and the men who tortured your mother, but I have nothing to prove it."

He pushed the journal across the table toward them. "I took the liberty of reading what your mother wrote about her pregnancy. I didn't see anything that would help in solving the case. When you go through it, you'll get a feel for what she went through and how much you all meant to her."

A heavy silence filled the room as all three women stared at the journal.

"I don't have any leads to follow up with. My boss wants me to reclose the case. I've documented everything I found and made you a copy of it. It's in the back of the journal. If you have any questions, I'll do my best to answer them. I've spent more time on this case than any other and regret not being able to solve it." He passed out cards with his contact information to all of them.

"This is a lot to swallow," Violet said. "Could we have a few days to go through everything?"

"That's fine. I'll keep your number in case anything comes up."

"Thank you for all you've done. We're very grateful." Lily's voice trembled.

"We plan to visit the hospital soon," Rose added, "to see where we were born. Do you know where she was buried?"

"The hospital has a graveyard on the grounds. Your mother was originally buried as Jane Doe. At my request, they're adding a new headstone. The inscription will read, 'In memory of Clara, the courageous mother of the Texas Flower Girl triplets.'"

"That's perfect. Thank you so much," Violet said quietly.

"I was at the hospital a couple of weeks ago, and the nurse who watched over you was there. Her name is Ann Parkinson. She gave me these." He reached into his briefcase.

"She made them for each of you during the weeks that you were at the hospital before your adoptions. She was quite fond of you."

He pulled a zip-lock bag out of his briefcase and handed it to Rose. "Nurse Parkinson obtained a piece of your mother's dress, laundered it, and made something for each of you to hold your pacifiers. She hoped you'd cherish them, coming from your mother and all. They had already nicknamed you the Flower Girls and named each of you for one of the flowers in the material. When you were adopted separately, they were left behind. She kept them in case you ever made it back. I think she was hoping she'd see you all again. She was shocked when I told her that none of your adoptive parents changed any of your names."

The women looked overwhelmed as they pulled out the mementos made for them.

"You have no idea how much we appreciate the time you've spent on our mother's case, Detective." Lily cleared her throat. "We'll never be able to thank you enough."

"Well, you got handed a raw deal right from the start, and I just couldn't let it go. Maybe this will bring some closure for me as well. Is there anything else?"

When they didn't seem to have any more questions for him, he escaped. It had been a tough night for the Flower

Girls of Texas. He hoped the joy they found together would help them cope and that the information he'd provided would answer at least some of their questions.

A sudden feeling of unease made the hairs on the back of his neck stand up as he drove home. He didn't want to mention it on top of everything else the women had to deal with, but the man who had kidnapped their mother was still unaccounted for.

CHAPTER 11

Revisiting the Past

Nurse Parkinson

When Ann Parkinson saw the three women come into the break room at the hospital, she started to cry. "You're the Flower Girls, aren't you? Detective Baxter called and gave me a heads-up that you might come by."

The girls nodded.

"Oh, my. You are all so beautiful. Rose, you still have your beautiful dark eyes and curls, and Violet, you kept the strawberry-blond hair. And Lily, you didn't have anything but blond fuzz when I saw you last. Come with me and let me show you around. There are several people who want to see you."

After they thanked her for making the mementos from their mother's dress and met some of the others who had been there when they were born, they asked Nurse Parkinson if they could see their mother's grave.

"Of course, we just got the new headstone put on. Detective Baxter paid for it out of his own pocket. He's such a nice man."

The graveyard wasn't far from the back of the hospital. It was quite small but neat as a pin. The three sisters stood before the gravestone in silence, arms around each other. Ann stepped back to give them privacy.

"Dear God," Lily prayed, "we are thankful for the strength you gave our mother to endure what she did to ensure our survival. We are humbled beyond words and look forward to thanking you and her when we get to heaven. Lord, please give her a big hug for us and let her know that her babies survived, against all odds. We ask this in your Son's holy name. Amen."

They hugged Ann and thanked her for caring for them until they were adopted.

"It was my honor. You are all just as precious as you were back then. Come back and visit any time. You are our Flower Girls, and you are always welcome here."

Lily

The three girls took a few days to pore over Clara's journal. Lily knew this was her biological mother, but it still seemed like a story about someone else. She was elated to have her sisters to share her thoughts with and was glad they were meeting at Rose's apartment above the shop. It would give them the privacy to be open about all of it, and she was ready to hear what the other two women thought.

"I'm proud of what she did to save us," Lily said as they all sat in Rose's apartment, sipping hot tea and nibbling on the cookies Rose's mom had provided. "Do you think she was saved? I hope so. I really want to meet her when I get to heaven. She worked so hard to make sure we were born, and I have to believe she's looking out for us now. Makes me feel like I have a guardian angel looking out for me from heaven, in addition to the one God sent me to be my mom here on earth."

Violet

"I know what you mean," Violet added. "I didn't have a dad growing up, but I had Grandpa Jonas and he was amazing. Grandma Marge was too. There was never a moment when I felt lonely or unloved. What I feel most about Clara is sadness. She lost everything. The writer in me wants to share this story so everyone knows the horror she was subjected to. It makes me shudder to think of those evil men getting away with it. By the way, what church do you and Mama Martino go to, Lily?"

"We attend the First Congregational Church here in Houston," Lily offered. "It's a bit smaller than most, but the pastor is a great speaker and watches over all of us. When I moved out of the Rhodes household, I needed someone to talk to, so I told him my story. It helped a lot. Of course Mom helped too. Violet, would you and your mom like to go with us this Sunday?"

"I'll talk to her and make sure it's okay, but I would like to try it."

"What about you, Rose? No pressure, but it won't be the same without you."

Rose

"We went to church when I lived at home," Rose said. "And I go with my parents when I visit. But I haven't taken the time to find a church here. It would be wonderful if we all went to the same one. I want to take a good look at how and what I believe. I know one thing for certain: divine intervention brought us together."

Rose put down her tea and leaned forward. "I think a lot of our sadness comes from not knowing our birth mother our whole lives. I mean, my mom and dad are the best parents ever, but thinking about Clara makes me want to weep for all she went through and lost. One thing is for sure. Finding the two of you and being able to share all this with you makes it easier for me. We really did beat the odds when we found each other. Let's continue to rejoice and thank God for that. And I'm definitely in favor of trying your church, and I know right where that one is. It's not far from here."

"Good. The V-girls will pick you up on our way," Violet offered.

The women loved being at church together, and Sundays became their day to see one another and have lunch together after. Mama Martino and Victoria became instant friends, and Rose's parents came with them often. Stevie and Antonio were considering changing churches so they could all worship together. All of their parents seemed to enjoy each other almost as much as the girls did.

After work one evening, the triplets were all at Violet's house and the subject of their moms came up.

"I have to say," Violet said, "it's wonderful to see our moms getting along. Did you know they all meet with a personal trainer at that small gym downtown? And last Wednesday, they had lunch at the Black Bear Diner."

Violet's mom came in, carrying fresh-baked brownies. "Does that surprise you, Vi? We like each other, and we all connect over watching our beautiful girls grow up. I have to tell you, it's wonderful having friends who instantly understand you."

"I get it. That's how I feel about Rose and Violet." Lily took a brownie off the plate that Victoria passed around. "These brownies are yummy, Mama V. But you have to stop feeding us or we're going to have to go to the gym with you."

"Nonsense. You girls are more slender than a willow branch. I know you all got that from your mama, God rest her soul."

Detective Baxter

Dan had closed the case of the Flower Girls, but he still thought about the three women. He wished he could find full closure on the case himself. It still bugged him that Macho Maxwell had not been found. He could only conclude that he was buried somewhere in Mexico in an unmarked grave.

One night, Dan came home from work after stopping at the market and was putting something in the garage refrigerator when he heard a noise. He felt for his gun, straining to see into the darkness. He saw a shadow out by his mailbox. It started coming closer.

"Identify yourself. Who are you?"

The shadow kept moving. As it came into the yard light, he pulled out his weapon. "Stay where you are! I'm a police officer and I have a gun."

The shadow stopped, and Dan could see it was a man as he stepped into the yard light. The man had a gun too, which was pointed directly at him. It was none other than Mr. Macho Maxwell.

"I've been waiting for the right moment to pay you back for almost getting me killed. Lucky for me, I was able to get rid of those other idiots. Since you made it through the accident, I still have to take care of you."

The accident? He must have been the other driver in his accident!

"You were involved in illegal activities. Heinous crimes against young pregnant girls, including stealing their babies and letting some of them die. You're looking at life, mister, so you might want to hand over your weapon before threatening a police officer is added to the long list of crimes you've committed."

"I'm not going anywhere, and neither are you." He pulled up his weapon to shoot at the same time Dan did. Two shots rang out. The shadow went down.

Searing pain plowed into Dan. The bullet hit him square in the chest and drove him to the ground.

CHAPTER 12

Case Solved

Donna Baxter

*D*onna watched the funeral procession make its way to the grave site. Three women stood at the front of the crowd, their parents behind them, while the flag on the casket was removed, folded, and handed to her. She knew who they were from her husband's description.

After a twenty-one-gun salute, she walked over and placed a red rose where the flag had been, then made her way back to her chair. A Scripture reading followed, and the casket was slowly lowered.

She stood as the Flower Girls—Lily, Violet, and Rose—walked over to her. Dan had shared their story over the years, and she loved them almost as much as he had. His cases were never just cases to him. Especially cases like theirs.

"We are so sorry for your loss, Mrs. Baxter. Your husband was a good man. We weren't even aware of the danger he took on while trying to solve our mother's case."

Violet stepped back and Rose moved forward. "It meant a lot, what he shared with us about our birth mother, but he kept the danger out of the story. We are very thankful, but we're here for you now, if there is anything we can do."

Lily came forward and took her hands. "I would like to pray for you, Mrs. Baxter. Is that okay?" At her tearful nod, Lily began. "Dear heavenly Father, we ask you to look after Mrs. Baxter as she grieves for her beloved husband. Watch over her, guide her and comfort her, and let her find strength in you as she goes forward. Her husband gave his life trying to make sure we were safe. I know you have a special place for people like Detective Baxter. Let the rest of us be forever grateful for his ultimate sacrifice. Amen." Lily dropped her hands, gave her a quick hug, and stepped back with her sisters.

"Thank you all for coming today. Dan would have been honored by all you have done. No one could keep that man from putting himself in danger for others. It's who he was." Overcome with emotion, she nodded to the girls and left, letting two of her close friends guide her back to the vehicle she had come in.

Case Solved

The triplets dropped flowers on the casket as they left. A bright pink rose, a bunch of violets, and a pure white lily.

The girls and their parents all gathered at Stevie and Antonio's home after the funeral. A light lunch awaited them, but no one felt hungry. A weighty silence filled the living room.

"What a courageous man." Antonio said at last.

Stevie nodded. "I'm thankful that other man's wickedness has been stopped. I just wish the detective didn't have to die to make it happen."

"Did any of you find out what happened to Maxwell?" Victoria asked.

"The article in the newspaper just said he died, but I don't think he ever made it to the hospital," Nanny said. "I have a friend who works in forensics. He told me the guy crawled as far as he could and died behind a garbage truck about a block away. Right where he belonged, I say. Just another piece of garbage."

"Mom!" Lily exclaimed.

"Well, child, I'm sorry, but it is what it is. That man had to be pure evil to be part of your mama's death and now Detective Baxter's too."

After lunch, everyone went their separate ways. The three sisters stood in the driveway talking.

"I know our lives started out with our mother's death," Violet said, "and that trying to solve the case brought death again. But I don't want that to be our legacy, do you?"

Rose put an arm around her. "I don't think it has to be about that at all. We can make a difference to those around us, take care of our families, and be there for each other always. Knowing I have you in my life brings a wondrous kind of joy. It's like being granted a miracle."

"That's right," Lily said, "and we have God to thank for it. He created us and kept us alive for a purpose. Going to church and praying means more because we're doing it together. We may have missed twenty-four years as sisters, but that should just make us more determined than ever to ensure that our faith is strong enough to get us through anything that happens . . . no matter what."

"No matter what," Violet echoed. "You know, I think I've just found the topic of my first story, and you two can help me. I want it to center on Clara's faith. I believe it's what got her through everything she experienced."

"We'll help." Rose and Lily joined hands, and Lily reached for Violet's. "We're the Flower Girls of Texas. All for one and one for all."

Violet laughed. "Now that we have each other, think of all we can accomplish to make this world a better place. I think that's just what God created us for."

Case Solved

"Amen," Lily added. "Amen."

And after one last group hug, the triplets set off to do just that.

CHAPTER 13

Clara's Story

Written by Violet Taylor, in collaboration with
Lily Martino and Rose Cortez

This story is dedicated to Detective Dan Baxter, who refused to give up, and Clara, the courageous mother of the Texas Flower Girl triplets.

Clara looked around the office as she waited for her name to be called. She still couldn't believe she was pregnant. After her husband left, she'd thought her life was over. Christopher hadn't been keen on having her eggs fertilized outside of her body before being implanted, but he had finally gone along with it. It was their last chance of having a baby using her eggs, and he couldn't deny the fact that he tested sterile. Using donor sperm to fertilize eggs, the doctor had assured them, happens more often than people realize.

Twice she had been implanted with two of the fertilized eggs, and twice she had lost them within a couple of weeks. There were only three left.

In the midst of going through the fertilization process, Christopher made plans to return to Russia. He told Clara his mother was sick and he had to go care for her. She was exhausted with all the preparations for fertilization and hadn't noticed items were missing from the house. When he left, and she finally put it together, she discovered he had emptied their joint bank account and tried to get into the trust fund she had inherited from her grandmother. Thankfully, his ID was not in their system, and her grandmother had made it available to only her . . . or her offspring in the event she had children. He had to settle for a diamond ring and necklace that had belonged to her and whatever items he could turn into quick cash.

When she tried to have him investigated, his name couldn't be found in the records. There were lots of Christopher Clarks, but none who matched the one she had married. The detective told her she was wasting her money, as it probably wasn't even his real name.

Devastated for months after her husband left, and wishing desperately for a child to devote herself to, Clara had made an appointment with her doctor.

"I know you want a baby, Clara, but the emotional trauma you've gone through might affect you getting pregnant."

"I understand. We paid for three attempts, and this will be the last one. I'd like you to implant all three of the fertilized eggs that are left. Let's pray that at least one of them will survive."

She waited alone every day, expecting to feel the pain and rush of blood she had experienced the last time. She prayed endlessly, begging God to give her this one last blessing . . . a child of her own.

She and Chris had moved to Texas after impulsively getting married one evening. They had a few friends but no real family, as Clara's grandma had recently passed and Christopher's were in Russia. This was supposed to be a fresh start . . . just the two of them. No one knew them in Texas, and they would make a family and new friends together. Chris made it sound so exciting. Clara knew now that her husband had been nothing but a con artist.

No one knew her or what she had gone through except Janice, who worked at the small library in town and was also pregnant. When Clara went to the library seeking something to read that would pass the time while she waited for her babies, she gained a friend along with books. She had always loved reading, but having a new friend brought her more comfort than she thought possible.

Three months later, all three embryos seemed to be developing normally.

"Clara?"

Standing, she made her way to the assistant who had called her name and followed her to an examination room, where she was weighed and told to wait for her doctor.

With a light tap on the door, the doctor entered the room. "Sorry for the wait. Busy day." She washed her hands and dried them thoroughly. "How are you, Clara?"

"Pretty good. The nausea is only occasional these days, and I'm still a little tired. But I haven't had any signs of bleeding or cramps. That's good, right?"

"Yes, it is. You are starting to look pregnant, and your weight gain is normal for carrying multiples. But I'd like to do another ultrasound to see how everything looks."

As she was prepared for the ultrasound, Clara said a little prayer that the babies were all doing well. She watched the screen intently, looking for any signs that might cause concern.

"You can see the three embryos pretty clearly. The separate gestational sacs tell me they will be fraternal triplets. Even though they are close together, I can hear three distinct heartbeats. Would you like to listen?" The doctor handed Clara the headphones.

As she listened to the heartbeats, she wondered whether they were girls or boys. "Is it possible to tell the sex yet?"

"Well, I can give you my educated guess. I could be missing something at this stage, but I'm pretty sure all three are girls."

Clara left the office on cloud nine. She had to be careful for the next five or six months or she could still lose her baby girls, but she wasn't worried. She had relied on her faith to get her through the awful months after Chris left, and she felt closer to God than she ever had.

She would be fine financially, thanks to her grandmother. She could focus on her babies without money concerns for a long time.

Stopping for frozen yogurt on her way home seemed like the perfect way to celebrate being three months pregnant. At four months, she celebrated with three mini pineapple upside-down cakes, one for each of her girls. At six months, now officially able to deliver early if necessary, she ate a whole container of frozen strawberries.

Only three more months to go to carry all three babies for the full nine months, though her doctor assured her it was perfectly normal to go into labor a month or more early with triplets.

Clara had carefully documented her entire pregnancy. At first she thought it might help her notice any signs of losing them, but after a few months, it became a legacy of love. She spilled out her tale about Christopher, telling them she had more than enough love for all three of them and always would. She mentioned her friendship with Janice and some of her favorite things. She shared that she had decided to see what each of them looked like and would name each of them as she held them in her arms.

On June 2, 2001, Clara waddled into the library to compare journals with Janice. Seeing her friend at the desk, she hurried over. Janice had mentioned she wanted to see the kinds of things Clara had included in her journal.

"Hi, Clara. Any time now, right?"

"Yep. I still have a few weeks till I'm full term, but it feels like they could come at any minute. I just finished the three blankets I've been crocheting and wanted to show you my journal before I go into labor. How's yours going?"

"It's fine. But I was hoping to read some of the things you captured to make sure I'm on track. I just hit my six-month mark, and I can't wait to see my little man."

"I'll bet Jared is over the moon about having a boy."

Janice put her arm around Clara. "I know life hasn't been easy since Christopher left, but soon you'll have three precious little girls to share your life with. Hey, will you sit here behind the desk for a few minutes while I use the restroom and grab a snack? It seems like I'm doing one or the other all the time now. And see that man over by the window? He's been here a while and keeps looking at me. I've seen him in here before, but he never checks out books. He's kind of creepy."

Clara watched her walk through the door to the restroom, not really worried about the man. Looking through her journal, she marveled at the stages she had documented. Since it was almost closing time, she hoped Janice would accompany her to the café down the street so they could visit.

Suddenly, the man Janice had mentioned rushed behind the desk and grabbed her arm. Her journal went flying, almost hitting him in the face. When it hit the floor, he kicked it aside and pulled out a gun.

Janice came out of the restroom and headed her way, waving her arms. "Hey, mister, what are you doing?"

The man shot her twice, once in the head and once in the chest.

Clara's body went numb. She tried to scream, but the man slapped his hand over her mouth. She looked around, but there was nobody else in the library at this late hour.

"If you want to live, go along with me, or you'll never see that baby you're carrying." He steered her toward the door, keeping so close to her she could feel the gun he had pressed back against her side. *Please God, don't let him hurt my babies.*

Once outside, he shoved her into the back of an SUV waiting at the curb. He jumped into the driver's seat, and she heard the click of the locks. She tried the handle but it didn't budge.

"I don't know what you want or where you're taking me, but if you don't stop and let me use a restroom, I'm going to pee all over your plush seats back here. I've heard that urine smell is really hard to get rid of."

The man cursed, but a few minutes later he pulled up to a run-down café. "You've got five minutes. You say one word and everyone inside will die."

He jumped out, came around, and jerked her out of the car, keeping a hold on her arm. He marched her inside and to the back. There was only one restroom. She went inside and did her business as quickly as she could. She didn't want to be the cause of anyone's death. The man was right beside her when she came out, marched her back outside, and shoved her into the car.

"You look obscene," he growled when he jumped back into the driver's seat. "How many babies are in there?"

"Three," she replied tersely. "Not that you care. Where are you taking me?"

"None of your business. Just keep quiet until we get there."

"Will you at least call an ambulance for my friend? Please?"

"Your friend is dead. She shouldn't have come out and yelled at me. She's the one I wanted. But no worries, sweetheart . . . you're three times better."

Exhausted by everything that had happened, Clara found herself unable to keep her eyes open. She awoke at the Mexican border, startled by the bright light and different voices.

"Finally. I wondered if you were going to make it or not. It's an hour past my shift." The man's voice was gruff and she could tell he wasn't happy.

"You're taking me to Mexico?" she almost shouted.

"I said be quiet," the driver hissed at her. Turning back to the border official, he changed his tone. "Yeah, a little tougher than I thought it'd be."

"No way," Clara shouted. "You let me out of this car right now. Help!"

The gate went up, and they were on their way. Then the car stopped abruptly. "Shut up. One more noise and that pretty little face of yours is going to be rearranged. Probably will be anyway."

Clara sobbed. Her anxiety must be making its way to her babies, because they were moving in every direction. She tried to calm down and watch out the window to see where he was taking her, but it was totally dark outside.

She prayed for strength to get through whatever awaited her. *Heavenly Father, be with me now and help me persevere through whatever unfolds. I am your daughter, Lord, and I love you with all my heart, but I am worried and scared. I pray you will lessen my burden and see me through whatever comes next. Above all else, please keep these precious babies safe until they are born.*

When they finally stopped and the doors unlocked, she almost tumbled out the door, only to be hauled up by the man from the library. She screamed, but looking around her, she saw why it didn't concern him. They were in the middle of a forest.

As he turned her and gave her a little push, she saw the outline of a building. A door opened and two men came out.

"Well, isn't she a beauty?" one of them said. He had greasy hair and a scar down one side of his face. He walked over to her and pulled one of her golden ringlets.

"This one is carrying triplets. That should more than cover what I promised you. Give me my split and I'm out of here."

"Hey, Tommy, get Max his money and walk him to his car. You know where it is." He winked at the third man, and Max followed him to the garage.

"Let's get you settled, sweetheart." He jerked Clara inside. Each of the men took an elbow and all but carried her down a flight of stairs. The second man was just as greasy looking as the first and was missing half of his crooked yellow teeth.

They entered a dark, dingy room. The two men set her on a chair in the middle of the room and secured both of her feet to the legs of the chair, then pulled her arms behind her and secured them as well. She felt one of her shoulders pop, and the pain as they stretched her arms behind her was excruciating.

"My babies are due to be born any time. Please, you have to help me."

The man who'd done most of the talking upstairs slapped her so hard across the face that she felt blood trickling down from the corner of her mouth. Shocked at the pain, she screamed. The other man punched her.

"Where does Max live?" the first man snarled. "We know he runs a business in the States. Where is it?"

When she didn't give them the answer they wanted, the second man burned her with the end of a cigarette.

Clara was in so much pain her whole body shook. She couldn't make them understand that she didn't know the man.

Just when she thought she couldn't bear another second, the pain stopped and she heard a voice in her head. *I've got you, Clara. It's okay. Close your eyes and let me take the pain for you.*

She closed her eyes. Suddenly she felt an aura of warmth and calm like she had never experienced. It seemed to wrap around her. She didn't want to open her eyes, even when the men screamed at her. When one of them punched her in the eye, she didn't register the pain or feel it swelling shut.

"Hey, boss," the third man shouted from upstairs, "he's getting away! Hurry! Get up here!" Without another look at her, the other two ran for the stairs.

Clara's head drooped forward. "No more. Please."

"Wake up." The woman's voice seemed to come out of nowhere. "We have to go now or they'll kill us both."

The woman's face came into focus in front of her.

"Okay, you're untied. Can you stand up with my help?"

Clara nodded, but when she tried to stand, she found out how weak she had become. The woman practically dragged her out the door.

Clara's Story

Once again, the aura she had felt in the basement engulfed her. She felt like she was watching what was happening instead of physically experiencing it. She half sat, half lay on something hard and cold, holding on to the side rail as it flew over ruts and limbs on the path. Then she was in a vehicle. She thought they would crash at any moment, but they finally made it to the hospital.

The driver got out, came around, and opened her door. The woman pulled Clara out of the back seat and walked her to sidewalk in front of the emergency room.

"Clara, you have to do this last bit by yourself. Do you understand?"

Clara nodded, but the pain was excruciating.

"You can do it," the woman said. She jumped back into the car and drove away. Clara fell to her knees.

You can do it, another voice murmured. *I am here with you. We will save your babies, Clara. You just have to get inside the doors.*

She looked around and saw no one near, but somehow she managed to crawl to the doors. They opened, and she made a valiant effort to stand and take a few steps.

"Please help me. Help my babies. They're triplets." She collapsed on the floor as a nurse ran toward her.

The warmth wrapped around her like a cocoon and the pain was gone. She floated above the scene, watching people hurry her to the operating room. The light was intense.

She watched each of her sweet baby girls as they were lifted out of her abused body. The doctor declared them a miracle. Then the scene faded, the light intensified, and she smiled as she reached out and Jesus took her hand.

Note from the Author

Dear reader,

I hope you enjoyed reading *The Flower Girls*. I wanted to write something a little different, and God kept putting the picture of baby triplets in my head. When I finally sat down to start writing, the story flowed out of me. That's how I know I'm on the right track . . . when I listen to God. He has been part of each of my stories.

The message I hope you will take from *The Flower Girls* is that God is always there for you, despite how unbearable life can seem. He has a wonderful plan for each of us if we listen and follow his Word.

Our world is a crazy place sometimes, and I hope you draw comfort and encouragement from reading this story. For descriptions of all my stories, visit www.jclafler.com.

Blessings,
J. C. Lafler

ORDER INFORMATION

REDEMPTION
P R E S S

To order additional copies of this book, please visit
www.redemption-press.com.
Also available at Christian bookstores, Amazon, and Barnes and Noble.

9 781951 310974